Molly tried to smile
through the pain.

"Oohh," she said as she pulled herself to her feet, "this will teach me not to slip and fall again."

Joseph scooped her into his arms, ignoring the look of shock on her face. "Where do we go from here?" he asked.

"How about to bed?" Molly asked.

"Sounds good to me," Joseph whispered, and watched with delight at the way her cheeks turned pink.

"That's not what I meant, and you know it."

He carried her through the house, set her in the middle of the bed, and then leaned forward, piercing her with a stare that sent shivers of excitement through her.

"Lady, this is the last time I put you in bed alone," he said softly. "Next time I have no intention of leaving."

Other Books by
Sharon Sala

CHANCE MCCALL
DEEP IN THE HEART
DIAMOND
LUCKY
SECOND CHANCES
QUEEN

SHARON
SALA

Finders Keepers

HarperTorch
An Imprint of HarperCollinsPublishers

❦

HARPERTORCH
An Imprint of HarperCollins*Publishers*
10 East 53rd Street
New York, New York 10022-5299

Copyright © 1997 by Sharon Sala
Excerpts copyright © 1993, 1996, 1997, 1999 by Sharon Sala
ISBN: 0-06-108390-9

First HarperTorch paperback printing: August 2003
First HarperCollins paperback printing: June 1997

HarperCollins ®, HarperTorch™, and ❦ ™ are trademarks of HarperCollins Publishers Inc.

Printed in the United States of America

Visit HarperTorch on the World Wide Web at www.harpercollins.com

10 9 8 7 6 5 4 3 2

⌒ *Prologue*

Molly Eden remembered screaming, then cradling her belly in a futile effort to protect the baby that was growing within. And then everything began to happen as if in slow motion. Although she and her fiancé, Duncan Wilder, were sliding sideways across the highway at a fast rate of speed, it seemed as if they were floating, and that the ice-covered tree silhouetted in their headlights was made of crystal.

Later, it would be the sleet peppering her face, the scream of an ambulance siren, and the blood all over her legs that told her she was still alive. As time would pass, she was to wish that she had not survived.

The room was warm, yet even in a drug-induced sleep, Molly shivered, reliving, over and over, the sequence of events that had cost her a child. Twice since coming out of surgery, she'd pleaded for someone to tell her of Duncan's fate. And both times, the answer had been circumvented until Molly was certain that, like her unborn baby, he, too, had perished. And then she heard him calling her name.

"Molly . . . Molly, can you hear me?"

Hovering on unconsciousness, Molly clung to the sound of his voice. It hurt to think, and it was oh, so difficult to talk, but the touch of his hand drew her closer and closer to awakening, and then finally she focused on the deep lines of concern upon his face.

It would be later before she would understand that something other than their baby's death had put them there.

"Duncan?"

"Molly . . . thank God," he whispered.

She focused her entire attention upon the broad shoulders and the familiar features of the man she loved, wondering as she stared if the baby would have looked like him.

"Duncan . . . the baby . . . we lost our baby." Tears slipped from beneath her lids, silent tracks of the depth of her despair.

"Tell her!"

A stranger's voice broke her concentration, and

for the first time, she saw that Duncan was not alone.

Duncan flushed, and looked away as Molly stared over his shoulder and into eyes filled with hate. The woman was tall, elegantly dressed in cashmere and fur, and obviously fighting the urge to speak for herself, yet Duncan's presence seemed to keep her slightly subdued.

"Duncan?"

Molly reached for the security of his hands, but when he moved out of her reach and stuffed them into the pockets of his slacks instead, panic began to surface.

"Tell her, or I will," the woman hissed.

"Tell me what?" Molly asked. "Who is she, Duncan? What can she possibly have to do with us?"

"She's my wife," Duncan said, unable to watch what he knew would be total, unrestrained shock upon Molly's face.

"No, dear God, no," Molly moaned, and covered her face with her hands.

"I didn't mean for it to go this far," Duncan said.

"What he means is, he didn't mean to get caught again," the woman snapped. "Or that you'd get yourself pregnant. You should have been more careful. The other love-struck college girls who fell for the handsome professor's line were smarter than you. All they got was an A in the class and then dumped. You, on the other hand, take the prize, sweetie."

Duncan spun. "Shut up, Claudia! Just shut the hell up! Molly was different!"

Claudia smirked. "Aren't they all?"

"Listen, Molly, I can . . ."

"Get out," Molly said, and clenched her teeth to keep from screaming. "Just get out of my sight."

"But you don't understand. We can—"

"There is no 'we,' " Molly whispered. "There's just you . . . and her. Now get out of my room."

Duncan dropped his head. "I'll pay for every-thing."

A sob slipped up and out of Molly's throat be-fore she could stop herself. But her eyes never wavered as she stared Duncan Wilder straight in the face.

"That's impossible," she said. "You can't pay for the baby I lost. And there's not enough money on earth to pay me for the fact that I can never have another child."

"Oh my God," Duncan said, imagining an im-pending lawsuit and the damage it would do to his reputation on campus. The dean would have a fit if he got wind of this. "I didn't know. Molly, listen, I'll make it worth your while to—"

Molly's gaze slid from Duncan to the woman behind him. "Get him out of my sight," she whispered.

For the first time since coming into the room, Claudia Wilder felt remorse. Once, Claudia had been just like Molly. Only she'd been Duncan's first student affair, and as a result, she was the one he'd married. And as she stayed with the philanderer who was her husband, she was the one who would suffer the longest. It was, however, her choice.

"Come on, Duncan. You've obviously outstayed your welcome."

They started out of the room, and then Duncan paused in the doorway, looked back, and shrugged.

"I'm really, really sorry."

The sheet wadded beneath her grip as she met him look for look.

"Yes, I can see that now," Molly said. The disgust in her voice was impossible to miss.

Only after the door had closed behind them did Molly give in to her grief. Everything, including her innocence, was gone.

5

ᥫ One

"Isth you my momma?"

Molly didn't know what startled her more, the unexpected question or the touch of a child's hand on her bare thigh.

"What in the world?"

She spun. The food on her barbecue and her solitary picnic were forgotten as she stared down in shock at the small boy who waited patiently for an answer to his question. She was startled by the unexpected pain of his innocent question—it had been years since she'd let herself think of being anyone's momma. But the child's expression was just short of panicked, and his hand was warm— so warm—upon her thigh; she couldn't ignore his plight just because of her old ghosts.

"Hey there, fella, where did you come from?"

Molly bent down, and when he offered no resistance, she lifted him into her arms.

But he had no answers for Molly, only an increase in the tug of his tongue against the thumb he had stuffed in his mouth. She smiled at his intense expression, and patted his chubby bare legs. Except for a pair of small red shorts, an expression was the *only* thing he was wearing.

His little brown belly was streaked with dirt, as was the rest of his body. Bits of mud and grass were caught between his toes, and hair two shades darker than his eyes stood every which way upon his head. The only thing clean about him was probably that thumb he kept stuck in his mouth.

"Where did you come from, sweetheart?"

His chin quivered and then he tugged a little faster upon his thumb.

It was obvious to Molly that the child was not going to be any help in locating missing parents. She turned, searching her spacious backyard for something or someone to explain the child's appearance, but nothing was obviously different from the way it had been for the last twenty-two years when her parents first moved in—except the child.

A car honked down the street, and two houses over, she could hear the sounds of kids playing in a backyard pool. However, from the looks of the dirt on this one, she doubted he'd recently been in any water.

"Isth you my momma?"

This time, his voice held a slight tremor as he slid a small, bare arm across the shoulder of her white halter top to secure himself more firmly within her grasp.

"Amazing! So that's how you do it."

Molly's remark was aimed at his ability to talk and suck his thumb at the same time.

"Are you lost, honey? Can't you find your mommy?"

His only response was a limpid look from chocolate-chip eyes that nearly melted her on the spot.

She frowned, patting his sticky back in a comforting but absent way and started toward the house to call the police when shouts from the yard next door made her pause.

"Joey! Joey, where are you? Answer me, son!"

Even through the eight-foot height of the thick yew hedge separating the homes, Molly could hear the man's panic. She looked down at the child in her arms and sighed with relief. If she wasn't mistaken, the missing parents were about to arrive, and from a surprise location. The house on the adjoining lot had been vacant for over a year, and she'd been unaware that anyone had moved next door.

"Hey! You over there . . . are you missing a small boy?"

"Yes . . . God, yes, please tell me you found him."

Molly smiled with relief as she realized her unexpected guest was about to be retrieved. "He's here!" she shouted again. "You can come around the hedge and then through the front door of my house. It's unlocked."

The thrashing sounds in the bushes next door ceased. Molly imagined she could hear his labored breathing as the man tried to regain a sense of stability in a world that had gone awry. But she knew it was not her imagination when she heard a long, slow, string of less-than-silent curses fill the air. Relief had obviously replaced the father's panic.

Molly raised her eyebrows at the man's colorful language, but got no response from the child in her arms. He didn't look too perturbed. But he did remove his thumb from his mouth long enough to remark, "My daddy," before stuffing it back in place.

"Well, really!" Molly said, more in shock for herself than for the child, who had obviously heard it all before.

She turned toward the patio door, expecting the arrival of just an ordinary man, and then found herself gaping at the male who bolted out of her door and onto her patio.

It had been a long time since she'd been struck dumb by a physical attraction, but it was there just the same, as blatant and shocking as it could possibly be. All she could think to do was take a deep breath to regain her equilibrium and then wave a welcome. That in itself took no effort, and it was much safer than the thoughts that came tumbling through her mind.

She saw the man pause on the threshold, as if taking a much-needed breath, and then swipe a shaky hand across his face. He was tall, muscular, and, oddly enough, quite wet. His hair lay black and seal-slick against his head like a short, dark cap, while droplets of water beaded across his shoulders.

He was nearly nude and his only attempt at modesty consisted of brief red jogging shorts that matched the ones the child was wearing. His pause was fleeting as he came toward her, his bare feet leaving a trail of wet footprints on the flagstone path as he ran.

Joseph Rossi had entered the woman's house without noticing its interior decor. All he could remember—all he could feel—was heart-stopping panic when he'd climbed out of his shower and realized his son was missing from his bed. Now, shaking with the sheer relief of knowing he'd been found, he wasn't prepared for the impact of seeing Joey's guardian angel.

Right at the moment, he felt as if he'd been poleaxed. The woman stood haloed in the intense glare of the setting sun behind them, and for a moment he could almost believe he was seeing an angel. She was tall and slim, and stood proudly erect, framed by the sun at her back and the cloud of auburn curls around her face. She smiled gently and seemed to hold out her hand. He blinked and then shuddered, remembering why he was here, and jumped off the patio and ran toward his son.

There was no mistaking the intense love in the man's eyes or the fact that the child went willingly from Molly to his father without looking back. And in that moment, when the child was lifted from her arms, Molly Eden felt oddly bereft and empty, and she winced, knowing that for her it would never be any other way.

"My God, Joey, you scared Daddy to death. Don't ever leave the house without me again, do you hear me?"

Joey nodded, then buried his face against his father's chest, suddenly shy at being reprimanded in front of a stranger.

11

Joseph hugged his small son tightly against his still-wet body, turning around and around in a circle until they were both dizzy and laughing.

Molly could only watch. The bond between them was obvious.

"We're making mud."

Joseph smiled at Molly, motioning apologetically to his wet body and Joey's dirty one.

Happy to be on the good side of right, Joey grinned and swiped his hand across his father's broad chest, leaving a tiny imprint of finger smears behind.

Molly shivered and wrapped her arms around herself to keep from joining in the fun. She'd always liked making mud pies—she'd just never considered making mud with a man before. The thought that had come to her was intriguing, and then shocking. What was she thinking? This man was her neighbor, and obviously married. Angry with herself for even considering falling into an old and painful trap, she looked away. It was then she remembered her grill. The wieners were creating a fire of their own.

"My hot dogs!" Molly made a dash for the grill.

My God! Joseph thought.

He stared at her backside and then tried not to. But it was an impossible task. Her long, tan legs made short work of the distance to the grill. He tried to remember his manners as he followed behind.

"I can't thank you enough, and although we haven't been formally introduced, at this point, an introduction is almost after the fact." He held out his hand. "Nevertheless, one Joseph Rossi is forever in your debt."

His dimpled grin made Molly forget what she'd been doing. Like a fool, she stood in the line of smoke from her grill, her eyes watering and choking instead of stepping out of the draft. It took several moments of uncomfortable silence before she could bring herself to speak.

"I'm Molly Eden. And I suppose that this dusty explorer is Joey." She tugged at the child's bare toes and stared at the matching dimples that came and went in his cheeks, too. *Like father . . . like son.*

Joseph pulled Joey's thumb from his mouth. "Joey, say hello."

Suddenly shy in the face of too many adult rules, he ducked his head and, when his father wasn't looking, slid his thumb back in his mouth. Joseph rolled his eyes, then flashed Molly another grin as he held out his hand.

"I owe you big time," he said.

All sorts of ways to claim repayment came instantly to mind. And because they had no business being there, she hated herself for the thoughts, and did not smile.

Joseph wrapped the child in another bear of a hug just because he could, and snuggled his nose against the child's dusty hair.

"You get another bath, boy. And this time, we'll do it together."

Molly tried not to think of baths and this nearly naked man all in the same thought, but it was no use. The only thing she could do to save her reputation was to turn back to the grill and her burned wieners and start talking.

"I had no idea that the house next door had sold. Although that could be because I'm hardly ever at my own home. I'm usually down at the Garden."

Joseph privately thought that whatever garden she was in could only be enhanced by her presence. He'd never seen anyone so enchanting, and decided that his son had good taste in women.

Molly turned, and this time managed a real smile as she held up two badly burned wieners on a long-handled fork.

"These don't look so good, but I have others. Why don't you and Joey go home, collect your wits and your wife, and come back for a welcome-to-the-neighborhood supper? I have plenty."

"No!"

The answer was too abrupt, and the frown on his face unexpected. Molly knew he was trying to make amends for his rudeness when he tacked on a "thanks," but the smile on his face had disappeared.

Well! He turned off the charm real fast.

Joseph realized he'd been rude, but short of explaining a miserable family history, which he had no intention of doing to a complete stranger, his best bet was to make as graceful an exit as possible.

"We've got to be going, and thanks again for finding my son. Is it okay to leave the same way I came in?"

"Yes, and as for rescuing Joey . . ." She resisted the urge to brush a dusty lock of hair from the child's eyes. "It was my pleasure."

Moments later she was alone and looking down at her burned supper. She made a face, then tossed the lot into the garbage, and headed for the kitchen to make a peanut butter and jelly sandwich. After this, the idea of a solitary picnic had lost its appeal.

"Found momma?" Joey muttered, tugging at his father's hair to get his attention as they entered their own house.

Joseph stumbled. That he was in shock was putting it mildly. He looked down at the expression on his son's face. It was the last thing he'd ever expected to hear him say.

"No!" he said abruptly.

Joey's eyes grew wide at the tone of his father's voice. He stuffed his thumb back in his mouth and began to work it against his tongue in a tense, almost frantic movement.

Joseph softened the tone of voice and cupped the child's face with the palm of his hand. "She's not your momma, son. She's not your momma."

Joey frowned and looked back over his father's shoulder and out the window overlooking their front yard.

"*My* momma." His answer was as abrupt and distinct as his father's rebuttal. He glared at his father, as if daring him to argue.

Joseph grinned. His son's developing personality took some getting used to. Although he was going on three, it looked as if he was already going to be as single-minded and hardheaded as his old man.

"Come on, boy. Let's get cleaned up. We'll worry about mommas later."

It was hours later before it dawned on Molly that Joey had not asked *where* his mother was, but *if* she were his mother. The puzzle kept her awake until two in the morning. It was only by dogged determination and the knowledge that she had a busy day ahead of her that she finally closed her eyes, quit thinking of dark-haired men, and fell asleep. And when she did, she dreamed of little boys with sticky hands and kisses and never knew that she cried.

More than a week had passed since their ill-fated meeting, and in that time, Molly had yet to see sign of a Mrs. Rossi anywhere. Except for a brief glimpse of a silver-blue Cougar periodically turning in and out of the driveway next door, she'd seen nothing else of her new neighbors.

And, she kept reminding herself, after her initial reaction to Joseph Rossi, it was probably for the best. The last thing she wanted to do was even dream of another married man, although in her own behalf, she knew that it would never have happened the first time if she'd known the truth.

With one hand firmly on the steering wheel of her delivery van, she glanced down at her wristwatch, making a mental note to remind herself to take the Sixty-third Street exit off of the Centennial Expressway, and then swerved to dodge a cat who was trying to make its way across the freeway.

She grimaced, refusing to look in her rearview mirror to see if it had survived the crossing. In

17

Oklahoma City traffic, on a Friday afternoon and forty-five minutes before quitting time, the chances of that happening were slim to none.

One more delivery and then it's quits for the day, she reminded herself as she took the exit.

It wasn't often that Molly Eden made her own deliveries any more. As sole owner of a flourishing flower shop called the Garden of Eden, she had good, competent help in her store, as well as a regular delivery man on the payroll. But it was summer, and to accommodate the employees' vacations, Molly was putting in extra hours herself rather than hire temporary help.

She glanced at the rubber tree behind her, and breathed a sigh of relief as it rode out the sharp turn she'd been forced to make. The delivery van was equipped with safeguards to assure safe arrival of all sorts of plants and flowers. But there were still occasional accidents, and Molly would have hated to make the trip back to the shop to get a replacement this late in the day.

She pulled into the parking lot of the high-rise business complex, rechecked the address on the order sheet, and then jumped out and headed for the back door of the van. A few moments later, with the rubber tree firmly stationed on a small wheeled cart, Molly headed for the front door of the office building. The promise of getting out of this heat and into cool, air-conditioned comfort was what kept one foot moving in front of the other.

She went from the lobby directory to an elevator and punched the button, waiting for a car that would take her to the ninth floor and Red Earth Designs. Her luck was holding. When the car came, it was empty, giving her plenty of space in which to maneuver herself and the rubber tree.

The mirrored walls inside the elevator reflected her flushed face, weary eyes, wild curls, and the kelly green shirt and matching walking shorts that were the summer uniform for the Garden of Eden.

Before she had time to smooth her hair or catch her breath, the elevator came to a stop. She started moving before the doors were completely opened, anxious to get out before she and the tree were caught in the act of disembarking.

Red Earth . . . Red Earth.

She read sign after sign on door after door as she walked the length of a long, cool corridor. The wheels rolled silently along the carpeting, leaving behind small tracks in the thick pile. Once she glanced back to make certain that she wasn't leaving a trail of dirt and leaves, and nodded with satisfaction when she saw the hall was as clear behind as it was before her. As she rounded a corner she saw the door she'd been searching for. She pulled the cart to the side and blew a loose curl from her eyes as she leaned down to retie her shoelace. Good impressions were almost as important as good products. With that in mind, Molly opened the door. The receptionist who looked up frowned at Molly's unannounced arrival.

"I have a delivery from the Garden of Eden. It's the rubber tree you ordered. Where would you like me to put it?"

Marjorie Weeks frowned. This young woman's appearance had taken her aback. She'd expected the plant's delivery, but not the fact that it would be delivered by a nubile young thing who was, in her opinion, not fully clothed.

"Be careful," she snapped, as Molly started through the doorway with the cart. "I won't pay for damaged goods."

"Yes, ma'am," Molly said, trying to ignore the fact that the woman's frown was growing deeper by the moment, and wondered what she'd done to cause such anger.

"Just put it over there." Marjorie pointed toward a narrow wall space in the middle of a large band of windows. "And don't get dirt all over my carpet."

Molly smiled and nodded, and then rolled her

eyes when the woman wasn't looking. *Her carpet, indeed!* If she wasn't mistaken, this woman was nothing more than a receptionist—at the most, a secretary. She seriously doubted if she owned the darned building.

She pulled the cart around, then started to drag the potted rubber plant off the wagon and into place on the floor, moving her backside in rhythm to the motion of the pot as she slid it in place.

Joseph Rossi dumped a handful of papers into his briefcase, shoved a weary hand through his hair, slung his suit coat over his shoulder, and headed for the outer door to his office. He'd never been so ready for a Friday in his life.

The move from Mississippi to Oklahoma had been traumatic. Then losing Joey had set his teeth on edge for days. Trying to organize a new household and an office and find a competent day-care center all in one month had been, to say the least, a trying experience. He exited his office with one thing in mind. He had two days of freedom to be at home with his son.

"Mrs. Weeks, I'll be . . ."

What he'd been about to say was lost at the sight of the shapely green bottom turned toward him. Her upper body—and he was in no doubt that it was a her—was lost in the leafy branches of the huge plant she was unloading. If he was any judge of shape—and, as a skilled architect, he was—he decided that the rest of her would probably do, too.

"Here, let me help," he said, and dropped his coat and briefcase into Marjorie Weeks's hands, unaware of the flash of anger on her face as he did so.

"No need," Molly said, and quickly slid the plant into place. She stood and turned, started to dust her hands on her shorts, and then froze at the unexpected sight of the man in front of her.

"You!"

"Well . . . hello!" Joseph grinned in pleased surprise.

"My gosh! I almost didn't recognize you with your clothes on."

The minute Molly said it, she realized how it must sound, but it was too late to stop the angry flush of red on the secretary's cheeks or the laughter that bubbled out of Joseph's mouth. He took one look at the shock on Molly's face and then laughed until tears came.

"Oh Lord, I needed that," he muttered, when he could talk without laughing.

"Well, I darn sure could have done without it," Molly said, then blushed when her remark brought another round of chuckles.

22

Marjorie Weeks glared. She was furious. In her eyes, the flip little female was nothing more than an ugly reminder of the circumstances that had pushed her back into the workforce at the age of sixty-one. Her husband of thirty years had left her for a sweet young thing half his age. She'd gone from a matron of some standing in their social circle to an aging divorcée with few job skills and a growing hatred of women under the age of thirty.

"Well! I never!" Marjorie hissed, and dropped her boss's coat and briefcase onto the desk.

"Now, Marjorie . . . I didn't either." Joseph chuckled again and gave Molly a lingering look. "But don't think it hasn't crossed my mind."

Molly gasped as the laughter died inside of her. This man was unbelievable. Here he was, a married man, and flirting outrageously in front of his hired help as if the woman didn't exist. She smiled thinly, bit her tongue to keep from telling them both off, and tried to make a graceful exit.

But pulling an empty cart out a narrow doorway was not a simple task. The cart bumped both sides of the door, then ran over the back of her legs as well, before she managed to clear the opening. With head held high, she rounded the corner and headed for the elevator at the end of the hallway.

"Wait!" Joseph called, following in Molly's wake.

She yanked the cart to a halt, punched the DOWN button, and stared mutely up at the wall, refusing to look at him as she waited for the light above the door to come on.

"Wait." He slid between Molly and the door as he reached the elevator. "I haven't had a chance to really say thank you for finding Joey the other day. You can't know how frightened I was. One minute he was sound asleep on my bed, the next he was gone."

The mention of the child made her give. But only an inch. Reluctantly, Molly looked up, then watched the expression on his face darken as he continued.

"You know . . . a new house . . . in a strange neighborhood. These days you never know what can happen. Joey means everything to me."

Molly softened. She knew that the panic she'd witnessed on Joseph's face that day had been real. She relented enough to answer.

"It was my pleasure. I'm just thankful I was home, and I'm usually not at that time of day. Summer is my busy time."

Joseph vaguely remembered something about her working in the gardens, and today she'd delivered his plant. He came to a logical conclusion.

"So, you work at a florist?"

Molly nodded, then glanced back at the elevator and punched the button again, although she knew it was a futile thing to do. The last thing she wanted was to be standing here visiting with a man who was obviously willing to cheat on his wife.

"What's the name of the place?"

"The Garden of Eden, and I don't just work there, I practically live there. I own it. You know how it is, when it's yours, there's really no such thing as a day off."

Joseph reassessed his perception of this woman. So, his pretty new neighbor did more than look good in shorts and rescue small boys.

"Okay, Molly Eden, when you're not in the Garden, what do you do for fun?"

She frowned. She'd heard this come-on so many times it made her sick.

"I have friends. There's plenty to do in a city this size."

Joseph's gaze kept drifting away from her face to her slender, tanned figure.

Molly rolled her eyes. Men! They were all alike. She breathed a sigh of relief as the elevator "dinged" its arrival.

"My ride is here."

Joseph heard the elevator coming. Before he lost his chance and his nerve, he blurted out what had been on his mind ever since he'd followed her out of his office.

"Would you have dinner with me sometime?"

Disgust overwhelmed her. If she hadn't been in a public place, she might have given in to the urge she had to punch him in the nose.

"I don't go out with married men," she snapped. "I'm not that kind of woman." She was furious with herself for giving him the opening, and that her initial assessment of the man had been on target after all.

The elevator doors were standing open. Molly all but slung her cart inside and then followed, anxious to get away from the insult she'd just been dealt.

It took a moment for Joseph to get over the shock of her anger and then to realize that, from her point of view, it was more than justified. Just as the doors began to shut, he stepped into the opening, blocking it with outstretched arms and legs. The expression on his face went from teasing to tense as he answered quietly.

"I'm sorry as hell that I gave you the wrong impression. I'm not married, Molly." He took a deep breath, then stepped back out of the doorway. "I'm not that kind of man." The last thing he saw was the look of surprise spreading across her face as the doors slid shut between them.

Well, thank you for waiting until I'd made a fool of myself to tell me, Molly thought, then cursed herself all the way back to the florist shop where she came face to face with her assistant, Cora Tulius.

"I was beginning to worry about you," Cora said. "I was about to send Harry to look for you."

Molly shrugged as she shut the door and turned the lock, then swung the OPEN sign to CLOSED. She swiped a shaky hand across her face as she walked toward the counter where Cora was running the day's receipts.

Cora's husband, Harry, was busy sweeping up the floors and restocking the cooler where the flowers were kept for sale. The couple had worked for her since her first year in business, and now, after six years, they seemed almost like a second set of parents.

Cora handed Molly the day's totals and then grinned, waiting for the praise that never came.

"What's wrong with you?" Cora asked. "It's not often we run that much during mid-July. I thought you'd be excited." And then she noticed the pallor beneath the heat flush on Molly's face. "Did something happen?" She frowned and swiped a hand across Molly's forehead to test for unnecessary warmth. "I knew Harry should have made the deliveries. You didn't have a wreck or anything, did you?" She looked over Molly's shoulder toward the van parked in front of the store.

"No. Nothing like that. I just did something I wish I hadn't," she said.

Cora crossed her arms and waited like an anxious parent for Molly to confess.

"You've yet to do anything I'd consider foolish," Harry offered, as he patted Molly gently on the shoulder.

"So . . . what's the secret?" Cora persisted.

Molly sank down onto a tall stool behind the counter, buried her face in her hands, and groaned.

"You remember I told you that the house next door sold."

Cora nodded. "What's that got to—"

"Let her finish," Harry said, interrupting his wife before she had time to create a new and bigger argument.

"I turned down an offer to go to dinner with the man, and he's as close to a Mel Gibson lookalike as I'm ever going to get," Molly said.

"That's too bad," Harry said. "You don't go out enough as it is. If I was twenty-nine and single, you wouldn't catch me puttering around in my backyard every weekend like you do. You should go. It'll be good for you."

Cora frowned. "I thought you said that the man next door had children."

Molly nodded, then looked away.

"Then why are you regretting not dating the man? I'd have thought with your history, it would be the farthest thing from your mind."

"Cora!" Harry said, shocked at the abrupt way his wife had reminded Molly of past sins.

"It's okay," Molly said. "Cora's not saying anything I haven't already told myself." She hugged the older woman for assurance. "He says he's not married. I just don't know if I can believe him. It wouldn't be the first time I got burned for trusting the wrong man."

The bitter smile on Molly's face made Cora angry. "If he's lying to you, better to find out now, before it's too late," Cora warned.

Molly nodded, then glanced at the clock. "Why don't you two go on home? I'll lock up. Thanks for staying, and I'll see you tomorrow."

Cora hid her worries behind a quick hug just before Harry hustled her out the door.

Molly gathered up the bank bag for a night deposit and headed for her car, all the while, wondering what dinner—and other things—with Joseph Rossi would have been like.

✐ Two

A week came and went with no further contact between Molly and the hunk. She satisfied herself with an occasional glimpse of his car and a few regrets for what might have been. But there were too many skeletons in her past for her to dwell too long upon her missed chance.

Even if the man's eyes were the color of semi-sweet chocolate, rich, dark, and just as impenetrable. Even if he swore he wasn't "that kind of man" either. She gave up the dreams and concentrated on the facts. And the facts were, she was busy having one of the most hectic, but profitable, summers the shop had ever run.

Cora's shout echoed from the back room. "Molly, you'll have to get the phone. I'm up to my elbows in orchids."

Molly sighed and dropped her scissors. Dismayed, she watched the bow she'd been trying to tie come undone as she ran to answer the phone.

"Garden of Eden. May I help you?"

"Yes," a very familiar, very male voice said in a slow, Mississippi drawl. "If this is *the* Garden of Eden, then I need to speak to Eve. Is she there?"

Molly took a deep breath. She recognized this voice. She'd been hearing it in her sleep for several days now. And in spite of her reluctance to admit she was glad to hear it, she was thankful he couldn't see her expression. She would have hated for him to know she was smiling. Enjoying his own joke, he chuckled in her ear. She shivered, then perversely decided to play along.

"Well, sir, if you mean *the* Eve, then I'm sorry to say she's not. I hate to be the one to tell you . . . but I'm afraid I had to let Eve go. There was a, uh, slight infraction of the rules."

He chuckled again, and Molly's stomach jerked at the slow, sexy laugh that bounced across her eardrum. She closed her eyes, counted to ten, then gripped the phone a little tighter as the game played on.

"So, since Eve's not here, you'll have to settle for me."

"Lady, I'd settle for you any day," Joseph said, and then added before Molly had time to reject his statement outright, "And . . . I have a question. Do you make house calls?"

"Depends on whose house," Molly said.

Joseph's eyes narrowed at the sound of her voice. Blindly, he stared at the panorama beyond his office windows, unable to appreciate the fine landscaping or the beautiful day, and then he hid a sigh of frustration. He was going to have to remember to be careful around this woman. For some reason, she was antsy as a bee-stung bear around men.

"I guess I should identify myself. This is Joseph Rossi."

"I knew that," Molly said, and then rolled her eyes at her stupidity. *Why don't I just tell him I'm interested and get this chitchat over with?* But her instinct for survival held her tongue, and so she waited for his response.

He grinned. *So . . . you recognize my voice?* That was an interesting fact to consider. "Could you come to my office?"

"What's wrong?" Molly asked.

"I think I have a sick tree."

Molly glanced at her watch. "The one I delivered? Gee, that's too bad. Hang on and let me check," she said, then covered the phone. "Cora, do you think you can handle the shop alone for an hour or so? We've had a complaint about that rubber tree I delivered over on Sixty-third Street last week."

Cora's eyebrows rose. She remembered more than the location of the delivery. She distinctly remembered that Molly's neighbor was the recipient of the tree.

"No problem," Cora said, and then waggled her finger to remind Molly to be careful.

Molly made a face and stuck out her tongue, and then uncovered the phone.

"Thanks for holding," she said. "We always guarantee our stock, and on an order that size, I have no problem with checking it out in person. I'll be right there."

"Good," Joseph said. "I'll be waiting."

He'll be waiting? For what?

Molly shivered as he disconnected. She shrugged out of her smock, grabbed her purse, and headed for the van. It didn't take long to make the drive from her shop on Pennsylvania Avenue to his office. In less than fifteen minutes she pulled into the parking lot of the high-rise and exited on the run.

"What am I doing?" she muttered, as the elevator doors slid shut behind her and she glared at her own reflection. "Stop running, calm down, and act like this is no big deal."

But her flushed face, wayward curls, and the

loud thud of her heartbeat told her otherwise. The elevator opened its doors and spit Molly out into the corridor with little regard for her nervous anticipation. It had places to go and people to retrieve.

Marjorie Weeks looked up from her desk and managed a formal smile at the young woman who entered the offices of Red Earth Designs.

"Well," she said shortly. "I didn't think they'd send just a delivery person. I expected someone more . . . knowledgeable."

"Hello, it's nice to see you again, too," Molly said sweetly. "And I own the shop. I'm about the best you're going to get."

Marjorie huffed. If this snippet was telling the truth, then she definitely needed some instruction on how a proper business owner dressed. In her estimation, this constant appearance in brief attire was not seemly.

"So," Molly continued, as she considered the source and ignored the snub, "what seems to be the problem?"

Marjorie pointed. "It's that tree you delivered. The leaves are beginning to turn, and some have even fallen off. You sold us a diseased plant, and I demand full restitution."

Joseph walked out of his office in the middle of his secretary's accusations and tried not to frown.

34

He knew quite a bit of Marjorie's personal history, and made it a point to overlook most of her assertive, possessive behavior concerning him and his business.

"That won't be necessary, Mrs. Weeks." The sound of his voice obviously surprised both women as they spun toward him. "Let's hear Molly out first and then we'll decide what needs to be done."

Molly looked away, pretending great interest in the tree, and Mrs. Weeks looked down her nose in disgust, then relaxed as Joseph patted her gently on the shoulder.

"So, Molly, what seems to be the verdict?" Joseph asked.

"Give me a minute, okay?"

She knelt, sticking her fingers into the soil around the plant, then frowning at the soupy moisture content as a rush of very cool air from an overhead air conditioner vent coincided with a blast of heat off the massive wall of windows beside her. It was a simple diagnosis, and one she should have thought of when the tree had been delivered.

"Move it," she said.

Marjorie Weeks jumped, then took two steps backwards in reflex to what Molly ordered.

Molly's mouth twitched. She looked everywhere, and at everything, except the expression on Joseph's face. She knew if she did she would burst into laughter, and thereby earn even more of Marjorie Weeks's wrath.

"I'm sorry," Molly said, and started to explain further. "I didn't mean you, ma'am. I meant the plant."

Mrs. Weeks's face turned a bright red as she stared long and hard at Molly, daring her to add insult to injury by laughing in her face. When she did neither, she could only follow Molly's lead and try to ignore the situation. She cocked her head, pretending to absorb Molly's explanation, and all the while wishing her to parts unknown.

"It's in a bad location, and it's been watered too much," Molly continued. "It's too wet, too hot, and too cold, all at the same time. How about"— she looked a moment, choosing a corner close to the door and away from the intense heat of the wall of glass—"over there?"

Joseph wasn't blind to the undercurrents between the two women. And while he would never allow anyone to tell him how to run his business, he couldn't have cared less where the damned plant was put. What he did want was to mend some fences with his pretty new neighbor. He hated being thought of as a cheat. He'd had enough of dishonesty in his own life without lying to someone he'd just met. Wisely, he let the women settle the situation between themselves and stood aside, waiting for Mrs. Weeks to okay the decision.

Marjorie looked around the room, relishing the fact that it was solely up to her to prolong the decision. But even she could see the wisdom of the suggestion, and finally settled the issue by nodding her agreement.

"Great," Molly said. "I think you'll see a marked improvement after the new location." And then she added, "But don't hesitate to let me know if you don't."

"Indeed I will," Mrs. Weeks said. "I take care of my responsibilities."

"Yes, ma'am," Molly said, and bent down to grab hold of the pot, intent on scooting it to its new location.

"I'll get it," Joseph said. "It's too heavy for you."

"Oh! Mr. Rossi! You'll get yourself dirty," Mrs. Weeks argued. "You shouldn't bother yourself with such menial labor. Let her do it. It's why she came."

Joseph calmly ignored his secretary's fuss as he knelt in front of the rubber tree. He was eye level with Molly before he spoke.

"Is it?" he asked.

"Is it what?"

"Why you came?"

Her eyes widened at his audacity, and she forgot to breathe. Joseph got lost in eyes so blue they looked clear, then he blinked, believing that he could see his own reflection, and tried not to imagine how stormy her eyes might get when she was aroused with passion. He'd already seen them darken in anger and wondered if she kept them open when she made love, or if she closed them instead, leaving a man with nothing but the tentative flutter of those ridiculously long lashes.

Molly shuddered, tried not to focus on his less-than-subtle innuendo, and grabbed onto the pot.

"If you want to help, you pull, I'll push. Then neither of us will strain anything important."

He grinned and complied, and the tree was soon moved to a new location. As soon as it was in place, Molly felt the itch to leave.

"I'll be going now," she said, refusing to acknowledge his lingering interest. "Mr. Rossi, thank you for your business. Mrs. Weeks, it was nice to see you again. If you ever have need of our services, don't hesitate to give us a call."

Molly resisted the urge to run as she headed for the elevator. But she could have saved herself the haste, because once again, Joseph followed her down the hall.

"So, Molly Eden, dare I take the chance, and repeat my offer of dinner?"

Because she refused to stop, he followed her to the elevator, waiting for an answer he wasn't sure he'd get.

Molly punched the DOWN button and prayed for a speedy response.

"Well . . . are you going to keep me in suspense, or is this a brush-off and I'm just slow in getting the message? You'll have to tell me if it is. I've been out of the dating scene so long, I wouldn't know."

It was the defeat in his voice that got her attention. She turned and stared. "You're serious, aren't you?"

He nodded. "As serious as I can be, lady. Will you trust me?" The minute he spoke, her expression darkened. He figured it was a safe bet that somewhere along Molly's life, someone had badly betrayed her trust.

Finally she shrugged. "I just might. But no promises . . . not yet. And nothing more than dinner, okay?"

He grinned. "It's a deal. And just to prove what a gentleman I am about the whole deal, I'll even provide a chaperon. Course, he's not housebroken, and he does still spill milk into his food on occasion, and I'm having a hell of a time getting him to quit sucking his thumb, but he'll do in a pinch."

The description of his son's behavior and habits made Molly grin. "What time?"

"Seven okay?"

"I'll bring dessert," she offered. "Is the host or the chaperon allergic to anything important?"

He returned her smile. "Only rejections, Miss Molly. Only rejections."

The elevator dinged, and Molly entered, sharing the space with three elderly women and a man who reeked of garlic. In reflex, she wrinkled her nose, then out of the corner of her eye saw Joseph grin at her response. He didn't miss a thing, she thought, and that made her nervous. If he was that observant, she didn't want him guessing about her own attraction toward him. And then she sighed. There was no need to second-guess a man who was capable of reproducing himself as perfectly as Joseph Rossi had. A fleeting thought came and went as she wondered what Joey's mother had looked like. Whatever the child had inherited from her had nothing to do with actual physical characteristics. And then she wondered why she cared. They had nothing to do with her . . . nothing at all.

*   *   *

Molly paced her bedroom floor, going from closet to mirror and back again. She stared at her reflection in dismay and then licked her finger before pinching a wayward curl from her forehead, trying unsuccessfully to squelch its rebellion and shove it back into order beneath the tortoiseshell clasp in her hair. She turned first one way and then another, checking as she had twice in the last half-hour for signs of a drooping slip or an undone hem.

She made a face at her own reflection and turned away. There was no use searching for any more imperfections. She was as ready as she'd ever be. Now she had to make a choice: Either call Joseph Rossi and make her excuses or show up next door and see if the man was as honest as he seemed.

But in her heart, the choice was already made, because Molly desperately wanted to believe. She grabbed her purse and the carton of strawberry ice cream and started down the sidewalk. It took less than a minute to get to his front door. It took longer than that before she got up the nerve to knock.

Just when she started to make a fist, the door opened. It startled her so that she took a step backward and almost fell off the front step and into the shrubbery.

* * *

Joseph watched her coming up the walk, clutching a carton of ice cream in front of her blue dress like a torch, and then waited anxiously on the other side of the door for her knock. When it didn't come as soon as expected, his impatience got the better of him. He yanked the door open, half expecting to see her running away. When she suddenly began teetering on the edge of his step, he realized that he'd scared the hell out of her instead.

With no time to think, he reached out, catching her just before she landed in his bushes, then pulled her back onto her feet, making no attempt to ignore the fact that her face had turned bright pink.

"Great entrance," he said, and bowed elaborately, as he stepped aside to let her make her own way into his home.

Molly's gaze was steadfast as she entered with her head held high. She refused to be embarrassed about an already embarrassing situation, and began brushing at unseen bits of nothing on the front of her skirt as she handed him the melting container of ice cream.

"Thank you," she said primly. "It was one of my better efforts."

Joseph laughed and Molly turned and stared, amazed by his ability to enjoy the simplest of things, even if it seemed to be constantly at her expense.

"Momma!"

Joey burst through the doorway on the run, a look of intense surprise and excitement spreading across his face, and then he stopped short, suddenly shy.

Joseph groaned, and muttered low so that only Molly could hear. "I swear this is not my idea. I've talked until I'm blue in the face, and he still seems bent on claiming you." He hesitated and then added with a teasing smile. "Although I honestly can't fault him in his choice."

Molly blushed, ignored the father, and knelt until she was eye level with the son.

"Hello, Joey." She offered her hand, thinking he would shake it. But he simply smiled and walked into her arms for a hug instead, bringing tears to her eyes as he wrapped himself around her neck.

"Found Momma," he told his father, then wiggled to be turned loose. "I show you my toys," he announced, taking Molly by the hand in a proprietary manner and starting to lead her out of the room.

Joseph grinned. "Better watch him. He's precocious, you know. That's a toddler version of 'want to see my etchings?' "

It was Molly's turn to laugh, and she surprised

herself when she did. She let Joey lead her away and missed the look of intense longing that swept across Joseph's face.

"Oh, hell, Joey," Joseph said to himself. "What have you done to our lives?" He looked down at the melting ice cream and headed for the freezer.

The move he'd made from Mississippi to Oklahoma had been partly a career choice and partly an opportunity to get as far away from the remnants of his old life as possible. Now here he was, making the first moves toward starting a new relationship when he'd barely gotten over the war wounds from the old.

"Daddy!" The excited shout from the back of the house jolted Joseph from his reverie and sent him hurrying to answer the summons.

He walked into his son's room and then stopped short, oddly jealous of how easily Joey had accepted this woman into his life. But the sight of Joey and Molly astride the horse he'd confiscated from a carnival's merry-go-round and installed permanently in a corner of the room was too endearing to ignore. Hell! If Molly would put her arms as tightly around him as she had his son, he'd be smiling too.

"This is great!" Molly said. "Where on earth did you find it?"

Joseph shrugged and tried not to stare at how far her skirt had hitched up her thighs.

"Wanna ride, Daddy?" Joey kicked at the horse's sides as if urging him on to great strides.

"I'd love to ride with you . . . and Molly." His voice lingered a little too long on the thought for her comfort. "But I think I'd better go check the spaghetti instead."

They didn't even know when he left the room. The last thing he saw was Joey leaning back against Molly's breasts as he looked up in laughter, and Molly smiling down at the dark head cradled against her chest.

Joseph sighed. "I think I've just been rejected in favor of my own son." He didn't know whether to be glad that Molly was so comfortable around children or sorry that she was so uncomfortable around him. He had thought that when the earlier confusion about his marital state was cleared up, she'd be fine. Obviously he was wrong. He made up his mind that before the night was over, he'd find out why Molly Eden was distrustful of men. It was easier said than done.

Getting through the meal was an eye-opener for Molly. Watching how calmly Joseph dealt with his son's drips and spills and requests for more told her what mere words could never have done. The man had the patience of a saint—and, from her point of view, an iron constitution.

Joey had reached a stage in his development in which he needed to see, from time to time, exactly what he was chewing. Obviously, from his point of view, there was only one way to do so, and that was to spit it out and check it for questionable contents.

The first time he'd done so, Joseph had looked nervously at Molly, waiting for her to shriek or gag. She'd done neither, although the level of her eyebrows had gone from normal to hairline height in the space of one second.

Molly had seen the dismay on Joseph's face and the intense concentration on Joey's. Wisely, she'd ducked her head and begun a dissection of her own food rather than burst into laughter.

"It's easier to see what's in there if you don't put it in your mouth first," Molly said calmly, picking through her pasta with delicate movement. "I personally like the little green things in the sauce, don't you? Cora says they make my eyes blue."

"Cowa?"

"Cora," Molly corrected him. "She's my friend. Maybe you can meet her sometime."

Joey nodded and then began taking careful note of Molly's bright blue eyes as well as the food that she'd wisely separated on her plate. It was the last time he chewed first and spit later. And it was the first thing Joseph thanked her for after Joey went to bed.

"You have an amazing way with kids," he said. "All easy . . . and natural. You don't make things too complicated or fussy."

Molly smiled at his compliment, ignoring an old pain at the thought of never having any of her own, and settled a little deeper into the easy chair in which she was sitting.

Joseph returned the smile and tried not to stare at the way her mouth turned up at the corners when she talked or the way she often put a hand to her breast when telling something dramatic or funny. He leaned forward, resting his elbows on his knees as he listened to her tell about the hell of making floral deliveries on Mother's Day, and made fists of his hands to keep from putting them on her. It was too soon, and maybe the attraction between them was wrong. But for Joseph, the wanting was already there.

"Maybe one day you'll be making Mother's Day deliveries to yourself and you'll appreciate it a little more," Joseph teased.

The smile slid off her face. She felt it falling and did everything she knew to keep it from happening, right down to a swift, sharp, intake of breath to hold it in place. It didn't work.

"What?" Joseph said. "What did I say?"

Molly shrugged and looked down at the floor and then back up at a spot just over Joseph's shoulder. There was never a good time to say this, but maybe now—before it could possibly matter, before they did something stupid by getting involved—now was the time to get it said.

"It's nothing."

The wound was old and healed, but the pain had never really gone away. She hated herself when she was unable to stop the tremble in her voice. She blinked, hoping that the tears stinging her eyelids would not show. "You had no way of knowing."

Joseph's stomach tilted. The pain on her face was obvious, and the way her voice was shaking made him sick. He'd have given anything to take back whatever it was he'd said.

"Knowing what, Molly?"

She shrugged, fiddling with the hair clasp on her head to keep from burying her face in her hands.

"I can't have any more children," she said.

It was the word *more* that made him shudder. That meant once upon a time there *had* been a child. He wasn't certain he wanted to hear what happened. Visions of his own hell kept knocking at the walls behind which he'd left it.

He sat upright, unaware that his eyes had narrowed and his mouth thinned. Unaware that he seemed to brace himself for something ugly, something he didn't want to face. Not from her.

Molly looked up and tried to smile. But the look on his face sent the thought into hiding. *Oh, dear.*

"Do you want to continue?"

She nodded. "I was twenty years old. A third-year college student, and madly in love with one of the junior professors on campus. We dated for nearly six months before I . . . before we . . ." She swallowed harshly, then shrugged as she fidgeted with the hem of her skirt. "I loved him," she finally said.

Joseph nodded. He could understand love.

Molly took a deep breath, because the rest of the telling came slow, and it came in agonizing clumps of words. "I got pregnant. It was an accident."

Joseph's nostrils flared, and for a moment, he could feel himself physically taking her by the shoulders and tossing her from his house. He knew—he could feel—what was coming. And to hear it again, from her lips, was going to make him sick.

"And just what did you do with that accident?" The bitterness in Joseph's words was harsh and ugly.

Molly jerked. The anger in his voice had nothing to do with her story. That much she knew. She took a breath and continued.

"I went to school . . . and I waited anxiously for her to be born."

The breath slid out of him like air escaping from a punctured balloon. The fire in his eyes dampened, and the lines around his mouth softened.

"What happened, Molly?" he asked.

Her chin began to shake. She took a fistful of skirt in each hand and looked down at the floor as the rest of her story fell out into the silence between them.

"He wasn't happy . . . but he didn't demand I . . . he didn't say I had to . . . Oh God! There's no easy way to say this. We had a wreck. I was five months pregnant and I lost the baby. I can't have any more children and that's that."

Tears slid down her face in silent streams. There was too much pain from the telling to even allow a sob to escape. There was too much shame from the rest of the story to face looking at Joseph when she said it.

"That's tragic, honey," he said softly. "But it's not your fault. Didn't he understand that?"

"What you don't understand," Molly cried, "is that the first visitors I had when I woke up in the hospital were him and his wife. He was married . . . and I hadn't known! I swear to God."

Joseph came off the sofa in one motion. He stepped across the coffee table and pulled Molly out of the chair and into his arms before she had time to catch her breath.

The tenderness and the strength with which he held her was the last straw. What was left of her composure disappeared about the time his arms slid around her shoulders. She was pressed against a wall of muscle and a swiftly beating heart before she had time to consider rejecting the comfort he offered.

"This is embarrassing. I didn't mean to fall apart." She wiggled, trying to pull herself out of his embrace.

"Hush," Joseph said, reasserted his hold on her, and rested his chin on the top of her hair, trying not to dwell on the shape of her next to the shape of him. "And I didn't mean to step on your ghosts. I've got enough of my own."

Molly heard what he said, knowing that what he'd just admitted was as much a warning as a consolation.

"Well," she said, trying to smile through tears. "I think I've just overstayed my welcome. Thanks for dinner, and tell Joey thanks for the ride."

"You don't have to leave yet," Joseph said, refusing to relinquish his hold, yet unwilling to admit to the comfort he felt in holding her against his chest.

"I think it's time all good girls were in bed," Molly said, and pushed herself out of Joseph's arms.

"That could be arranged," he said, teasing her with a practiced leer.

"You're going to deserve whatever troubles your son dumps in your lap during the next few years if you don't watch what you say around him," Molly warned.

"He's asleep," Joseph said. "He won't hear a thing."

"That's what my parents used to think. But I can remember faking sleep just to lie awake and listen to their laughter . . . and the secrets I imagined they were telling . . . and then the silence that always followed."

The image she'd painted of two people in love was staggering, and there was nothing left to say. The night was over, she was going home, and he knew it.

Why do I keep drawing out the need to say goodbye? What was so special about one woman that he couldn't even bring himself to say good night?

"See you around, neighbor," Molly said. "Next time, maybe the meal can be on me."

Joseph grinned. "As long as it's not burned wieners, you've got a deal." He slid a brotherly arm across her shoulder and walked her to the door.

"I'll call," he said.

"I'll answer," she replied. And then she was gone.

Joseph watched until he saw the light come on in her house next door, and then kept watching until sometime later when the lights went out. Only then did he give up his vigil, close the door, and go to his own room, and a lonely bed . . . and face the fact that he was falling for a temptress from the Garden of Eden.

∽ *Three*

Almost a month had come and gone since Molly had revealed her past to Joseph, and she still knew nothing about his. The vague references he made toward Joey's mother were anything but compliments. And while she knew little about Joseph, what she knew, she liked. He was a man who liked to touch, whether it was the curls around her face or the texture of her skin. He gave good hugs, and he loved his son and his job, and he liked to laugh.

Whatever he had left behind him in Mississippi seemed to still be there. He gave no indication of having brought any unfinished business with him. Not once during their frequent evenings together did he make even the vaguest of references to life before Joey. All Molly could do was hope and pray that someday Joey's mother didn't present herself in righteous indignation to reclaim her man and her child. And while she wondered and wished, she found her feelings for her next-door neighbors growing deeper and deeper.

Molly glanced up at the clock, muttering under her breath as she slipped a number six wire up through the base of a long-stemmed American Beauty. Her fingers flew as she wrapped it several times around the prickly stem to give it stability before clipping the excess wire from the end of the rose. With the skill that comes from years of repetition, she eyeballed the piece of florist's foam anchored to the bottom of a deep crystal bowl as well as the other twenty-three roses already in place, and slipped it into the perfect spot.

The arrangement was to be the centerpiece for a forty-fourth wedding anniversary dinner, and she wanted it to be special. The way Molly looked at it, anyone who could live with another human being for more than forty years and still smile deserved, at the very least, a decent bowl of flowers.

"Hey, Harry." She slipped an extra length of eucalyptus in between the two tallest roses. "It's ready for delivery, and just under the wire. Can you get to Nichols Hills before four?"

Harry swiped his hand across his balding head, looked down at his watch and then up at Molly, his eyes twinkling as he answered. "Are you willing to pay the traffic ticket?"

"No!"—she motioned toward the woman who was entering the front of the shop—"and neither is Cora."

"I'm not what?" Cora asked, then, with a thump and a grunt, set down the can of carnations that she was carrying.

"Never mind," Harry said, unwilling to let his wife into the discussion. If he really did get a ticket, he'd never hear the end of it. "I'm already gone. When I get back, I'll treat you both to dinner."

"Out to dinner? That sounds like bribery. Whatever it is you're apologizing for ahead of time, it won't work," Cora said, ignoring the twinkle in her husband's eyes.

Harry grumbled as Molly handed him the arrangement of roses. "Now see what you've gone and done. A man can't even be generous without having his motives questioned."

Molly ignored his acerbic remark as he grabbed the flowers and made a middle-aged dash toward the delivery van. She watched until he drove away before returning to her work. This couple were almost as dear to her as her own parents, and she privately thought they were enough like Fred and Ethel Mertz of the old *I Love Lucy* show to be their twins.

It was still painful to think of her mother's death and her father's remarriage, and even stranger to know that she had a nine-year-old half sister in the state of Washington whom she hardly knew.

The doorbell jingled, signaling the entrance of another customer. Wiping her hands, she turned to see Joseph entering her shop.

"Joseph!" The joy in her voice was just as vivid as the expression on her face, but the absence of his usual smile set her pulse to racing. "What's wrong? Has something happened to Joey?"

Joseph's heart skipped a beat. After what he'd just been through, the poignancy of her question caught him off guard. A woman he'd known less than six months was already more concerned with his son than Joey's own mother had ever been. He wondered what was wrong with him to have made such a mistake in judgment about a woman he thought he'd loved. But dwelling on past sins would do him no good, at least not today.

"No, he's fine. Although I need to talk to you and it indirectly involves him. Do you have a minute?" he asked.

Molly and Cora exchanged a look. Cora

quickly stepped into the awkward silence with an offer.

"I'm on the job, Molly. Besides, you need to take a break. Go get yourself something cold to drink at the deli across the street. You skipped lunch, remember?"

"Okay," Molly said, and let Joseph lead her out of the store and across the street, mimicking his silence until they'd seated themselves inside the corner booth of the deli. When the waitress disappeared with their orders, she leaned across the table.

"Now, what's all the mystery?"

Joseph frowned. It was difficult to find where to start.

"I just came from Joey's day-care center. It seems that the paperwork I filled out when I enrolled him doesn't jibe with what he's been saying."

Then he rolled his eyes, pinched the bridge of his nose to keep from cursing, and leaned back against the booth, staring at a point over her shoulder.

"And that was . . . ?" Getting Joseph to the beginning of a discussion was a lot more difficult than one would have imagined.

He leaned forward, suddenly ready to talk, then hesitated as the waitress slid their cold drinks in front of them along with a basket of tortilla chips and a big bowl of pico de gallo.

Molly lifted a warm chip from the basket, slid it into the thick, spicy sauce, and crunched. If it was going to take him this long to tell a story, she had no intentions of starving to death in the meantime.

Joseph stared at the way her tongue curled around the dripping sauce, then shifted uncomfortably in his seat as his body responded to her actions.

"Look," he said, shoving the chips to one side before he forgot why he'd come. "The bottom line is . . . when I filled out his papers, I told them Joey's mother was out of the picture, and that I had full and total custody—which, by the way, is true. The problem now is that it seems his only topic of conversation for the last few weeks has been his 'momma.' They've come to the conclusion that I've either kidnapped my own child or that I'm depriving him in some manner."

"Oh, Joseph! I'm sorry," Molly said. "What can I do?"

He looked away, almost afraid to ask. Joey had started this mess, but it was going to be up to Molly to get them out.

"I wondered if I could talk you into visiting the school with me . . . you know . . . sort of explain the situation and Joey's recent fixation? I know it's a lot to ask, but . . ."

"I'd be honored," Molly said.

"You would?"

"It would be my pleasure. There's only one catch."

A frown slid across his forehead.

"Can I please have my chips back first? I promise I'll eat fast."

He shoved the bowl of chips within her reach and then leaned against the booth and started to grin. The sick feeling that he'd been carrying all afternoon just disappeared along with the chip Molly stuffed in her mouth.

Within the hour, they were back on the road.

Joseph took the curve with one eye on the traffic entering the freeway on their right, and the other on the eighteen-wheeler trying to pass them on the left.

"Damn, I hate city traffic," he muttered.

Molly nodded in agreement, yet rode relaxed and confident that this man would get them where they needed to be as safely as possible.

"Joseph?"

"Hmm?" he answered absently.

"Exactly where *is* Joey's mother? I wouldn't have ever asked, except I've kind of gotten myself involved without meaning to. I feel like I need . . . no, I deserve an explanation. Do you understand?"

His fingers tightened on the steering wheel, and his chin jutted stubbornly as he dared one swift glance toward her face before resuming his keen eye on the traffic before them.

"For God's sake, don't apologize," he said. "After what I've just asked of you, I should have volunteered the information. It's just been so long since she was a part of my life that I often forget she exists. If it weren't for Joey, I probably already would have."

"Didn't you love her?"

The question startled him until he thought about it. It made sense considering the facts as Molly knew them.

"Once . . . I thought I'd never love anyone else. We were college sweethearts. We met in an English Lit class our freshman year. By the second year we'd moved in together. We made big plans and frequent love, and thought we were being very grown-up and careful." He sighed. "We were none of the above. She got pregnant."

"Were you mad at her? Is that what caused the breakup?"

Molly was relating to her own experiences, and Joseph knew it.

"No, honey," he said softly, unaware that he'd called her anything but Molly. But Molly heard it and wished for more. "I was shocked, but not mad. After all, I'd definitely participated in the procedure that had produced him."

Molly nodded, suddenly uncomfortable with the thought of Joseph and making love all in one sentence.

"So what happened?"

Joseph frowned, his anger suddenly renewed. "What happened was . . . while I was making plans to take a second job to pay for the bills, and trying to rearrange my schedule, Carly was making plans . . . without my knowledge . . . to have an abortion."

Molly gasped, but Joseph continued as if nothing had happened. He was too lost in old anger to relate to her or her feelings.

"I was in shock. I couldn't believe she wanted to kill something . . . ," he paused, considering his words, ". . . no, not a something, a someone, that we'd made from our love."

Molly nodded.

"I wanted our child." His fingers tightened on the steering wheel as he remembered. "Dear God, how I wanted it. I begged, I pleaded, I ordered. And then finally . . . we came to an understanding. If she carried the baby full-term and then gave him to me . . . I promised not to break her damned neck."

"Oh God," Molly whispered, unable to imagine a woman actually giving birth and then toss-ing away a child as easily as yesterday's news.

"So she agreed and Joey was born. To my knowledge, she didn't even care to hold him. She just signed the papers the lawyers had drawn up and walked out of our lives."

He slammed on the brakes and turned into the parking lot of Joey's day-care center, parked, then turned to face her, needing her to understand.

"Look, I'm not a fanatic. I do not judge other people, one way or the other, about their choices of having children. But this involved me, damn it, me! I lived in foster homes my entire life." His voice rose an octave as he tried to make Molly un-derstand. "I could never live with the knowledge that I'd let *my* child die because his birth was going to be an inconvenience."

Then he shrugged. "It was a good thing she disappeared so soon. I didn't have time to hate her and raise my son, too. Getting her out of my life was the best thing that happened to both of us. I just never realized that Joey missed the idea of having a mother. He's definitely not missed the real one. He never knew her."

Satisfied with the facts as she now knew them, Molly nodded. "So, come on," she said. "Let's go fix what ails Joey, okay?"

She started to slide out of the car when Joseph grasped her arm and stopped her progress.

"Molly . . . thanks," he said.

"Don't mention it," she answered, unable to face the full force of his stare.

Joseph cocked an eyebrow as he watched her get out from the seat without waiting for him to come around. She was still running from something. Could it be him? The idea was interesting, even intriguing, but it quickly disappeared in the wake of the seriousness of the issue at hand. He cupped her elbow, guiding her over the cracked pavement in the lot as they headed for the front door of the establishment.

Molly's stomach gave a half-hitch and then righted itself as she caught Joseph's smile. Nervous tension kept her from laughing this episode off completely. The sight of so many small children playing freely in the fenced yard beside the building reminded her that if her own baby had lived, she would have been seven, and possibly running and laughing in that very yard today.

"So, Mr. Rossi, I see you're back. Is this . . . ? Why, Molly Eden! I haven't seen you since the B and PW banquet last year. How are you doing?"

The Business and Professional Women's organization that Molly belonged to was about to be the best reference she could have had to back up her part in this misunderstanding.

"Lila! I wondered where you were working." Molly accepted, then returned, Lila Forshee's hug of welcome.

Lila nodded, looking a bit puzzled as she saw Molly's escort. "I'm the new site manager," she said. "I've been here a little over a year now. Do you and Mr. Rossi know each other?"

Molly grinned. "He's my new next-door neighbor. He bought the old Tussault house. You know . . . the one with that enormous yew hedge around it."

Lila looked at Joseph Rossi with renewed respect. She took her job seriously, and even the hint of a stolen or kidnapped child made her physically sick. Weeks ago, when Joey Rossi had started talking about his mother, she'd been suspicious, especially when the father had been so adamant that one didn't exist in their world. And then when the stories persisted, down to trips to Braums for ice cream cones, she began to worry. None of Joey's stories fit the facts. It had been her duty to investigate. But seeing Molly Eden, a woman she'd known most of her life, walk in with the man in question definitely added another shade of confusion.

"I've asked one of the girls to bring Joey in,"

Lila said. "I'm sorry, Mr. Rossi, but in this day and time, you surely understand my position."

It was difficult to face the full force of Joseph's angry glare, and Lila thankfully turned toward the doorway as she heard them coming down the hall beyond the door, yet when Joey arrived, his reaction was definitely unexpected.

"Momma!" Joey shrieked, and yanked away from the woman who was holding his hand as he made an excited dash toward Molly.

Molly grinned and knelt, scooping him into her arms before he knocked her off her feet. His hands were sticky and his face was streaked, but it was one of Molly's more memorable kisses as he wrapped his arms around her neck and hugged. The shock on Lila's face was impossible to miss as she invited them into her office.

Joseph scooped Joey up, then sat him on his knee, handing him his ring of keys to occupy his attention while he waited for Lila Forshee to start talking. But it was Molly who began to explain.

"I know I told you that Joseph was my new neighbor," Molly said, "but I didn't tell you that it was Joey I met first." She smiled at the child sitting in his father's lap, and then absently patted Joseph on the arm, unaware that the gentleness with which she'd included him in the moment touched him deeply. "Joey sort of . . . got himself lost and I found him. That was our introduction. And Joey has . . ." she paused, hoping Lila could read between the lines so she didn't have to go into detailed explanations in front of the child, ". . . well, Joey has sort of adopted me. He knows that my name is Molly. He knows that I don't live with them. But he refuses to call me anything but Momma. Frankly, Joseph and I have given up on correcting him. Joseph thinks that when Joey needs to let go of me, that he will. For now, if he needs to lay claim to something he doesn't have . . . I'm perfectly willing to be branded."

Joey giggled and crawled from his father to Molly, giving up the keys as he leaned against Molly's breasts. Inevitably, his thumb slipped into his mouth, and when no one seemed to object, he relaxed.

Molly looked at Lila, then smiled as she wrapped her arms around the child. "And I can't think of another thing I'd rather be called."

Joseph was too full of emotion to speak. He heard more than excuses and apologies for the innocent deception that they'd allowed his son. He would have sworn he heard Molly's heart breaking into very small, painful pieces. And he would have given anything to have her look at him with the same devotion that she gave his son without reservation. It was a joy and a misery all at the same time, knowing that the woman he was growing to depend on might love his son more than him. He didn't want to think about the fact that Molly might be using their relationship to get close to the child she could never have.

"Well!" Lila slapped her palms upon her desk. "As far as I'm concerned, this is explanation enough. I'm sorry I didn't understand the situation earlier, Mr. Rossi. Joey *is* at an impressionable age. Several of the children here have had birthdays during the last few months, and each time, one of their parents, usually the mother, has brought cookies or cake by to share with the children. I didn't realize that your son was feeling left out. I should have. I'm sorry."

Joseph stood, accepting the handshake Lila Forshee offered. "If his own father hadn't seen his need, why should you?" he said. "I'm through at the office for the day," he said. "I'll be taking Joey now. And the next time he comes up with new friends, we'll talk before we panic. Okay?"

"It's a deal," Lila said. "Molly—don't be such a stranger. Call me sometime, we'll do lunch."

Molly grinned. "Milk and cookies with all the trimmings?"

Lila laughed, then waved good-bye as the trio exited the center. And then she looked again, noticing the protective manner with which Molly was being escorted across the parking lot, and began to smile. It looked as if Joey wasn't the only Rossi interested in the next-door neighbor.

"I need to stop at the office and pick up some work," Joseph said. "Do you mind?"

She shook her head. "No, Cora's an old hand at emergencies. Besides, today was fairly slow. If I'm not back in time, they'll lock up."

Joseph handed her his car phone.

"Just to make sure, be my guest. It never hurts to check."

It didn't take long to issue the few orders necessary. By the time Molly was through talking to Cora, Joseph was pulling into the parking lot at his office building.

"I won't be long," he said. "Do you want to come up, or would you rather wait in the car? I can leave it running so that you two will be cool."

"Wanna go," Joey said, although his wishes had not been considered. "Wanna ride ina 'vator."

Joseph rolled his eyes.

"You know what?" Molly said. "I think I do, too. Let's go with Daddy. What do you say?"

"Yay!"

Joey's shriek was enough. Molly watched, her heart full of emotion, as Joseph laughed, scooped the child up onto his shoulders, and headed for the front door. It would have been obvious to a fool that they were crazy about each other. More than anything else in this world, Molly wanted a place in their lives, but after what she'd learned today, she wondered if Joseph Rossi would ever *really* trust another woman.

Marjorie Weeks's smile disappeared when she saw the woman who came in behind her boss and his son. It made her furious that this young chit was trying to insinuate herself into Mr. Rossi's life. It never occurred to Marjorie that she was imagining the relationship between Molly and Joseph. She saw him as a helpless victim and Molly as the conniving female. She would never have admitted that it was fabrication on her part and that she'd done nothing more than replay her own misfortune by substituting Molly for the woman who'd taken her man. She wouldn't see Molly as a reputable businesswoman. All she saw was a pretty face, a youthful body, and another man falling under the spell of lust.

"I'm through for the day," Joseph said, plunking Joey down onto the sofa in the waiting room. "You can lock up early, too, Mrs. Weeks. It's only an hour until quitting time. Put on the answering machine and we'll beat the rush-hour traffic. What do you say?"

She sniffed, glaring at the way the child kept

wrapping himself around Molly's long, bare legs. In her opinion, wearing shorts to work just wasn't seemly, no matter what the job. That they were nearly knee-length and anything but sexy didn't seem to matter to her.

"I don't mind staying," Marjorie said. "It's my duty."

Molly heard the censure in the secretary's voice, but refused to let it rankle. Today was too special to let some woman she barely knew bother her.

"I insist," Joseph said, and disappeared into his office. He came out moments later with a briefcase and a roll of drawings under his arm. "If you stay, then you'll make me feel guilty," he warned, flashing her a broad, engaging grin.

Marjorie wilted beneath the gaze. Even she was not immune to chocolate-chip eyes and wide smiles.

She shrugged. "If you insist."

Joseph grinned. "I do."

And then he stopped on his way out the door, suddenly remembering something he'd been meaning to do all week. "Oh, by the way, Molly, you need to give Mrs. Weeks your home phone number . . . just in case."

She nodded, remembering the talk they'd had one evening about putting her name on Joey's papers at the day-care center as someone else to call in case of emergency if Joseph was unavailable.

"Just in case of what?" Marjorie asked. The look she gave Molly was full of distrust and accusation.

"She's the other person on record at Joey's day care to be contacted if I can't be reached."

Marjorie's mouth pruned, her eyes glittered, her nostrils flared, but like the well-bred woman she was, she did nothing but reach for a pen and paper and then made note of the information and work schedule Molly gave her.

"If he had a mother, none of this would be necessary," she muttered.

Joseph heard and, after what he'd just been through, was less than kind in response to her interfering comments.

"You don't know what you're talking about, Mrs. Weeks. And until you do, it might be a good idea to keep your opinions to yourself."

High color slashed across her face, sweeping downward and disappearing beneath the ruff of lace at her neck.

"Yes, sir," she said stiffly, glaring fiercely at Molly, unwilling to lay blame on herself for her boss's condemnation.

Molly could only stare at the hate on the older woman's face. It made her sick, and it made her remember. The last time such a hateful expression had been directed her way, Claudia Wilder had been wearing it. It was a subdued trio that left the office.

Joseph felt Molly's dejection and wished that they were alone. But Joey wiggled to be put down, anxious to punch the button to the 'vator by himself. Dealing with the child kept Joseph and Molly from dealing with their own sets of feelings toward each other. That there *were* feelings, Joseph was certain. Just how deep—and for whom—was what remained to be seen.

Molly swept the last of the cut grass from the patio, thankful that for another week or so, her lawn was now down to an acceptable height, then rolled her shoulder and winced when a sore muscle twinged. It was a hazard people would never have suspected from the job that she did.

Being a florist was hectic, and often quite physical. Nearly everything was heavy or awkward, from handling long boxes of flowers packed in ice to juggling pots and pots of flowers that needed to be wrapped for resale. Having to come home and deal with a lawn and shrubbery was just adding insult to injury.

"Oh my gosh." She groaned and dumped the

last bit of cut grass into a bag to be disposed of later, then leaned against the handle of her yard rake.

"Hey, over there—are you all right?"

Joseph's voice surprised her. She walked over to the hedge, trying unsuccessfully to peer through the thick growth, and made a mental note that the thing needed trimming.

"I'm fine. What made you ask?"

"I heard you groan," Joseph said. "I thought maybe you'd hurt yourself."

"The only things that hurt are my feet," Molly said. "I hate to mow the lawn."

"Oh."

"What are you doing over there?" she asked.

"I'm . . . ouch!"

Molly grinned. She'd heard that particular curse before—and from this side of the hedge, if she remembered correctly.

Hearing Joseph's grunt, and then his short exchange of words with himself, made Molly grin. Joey had asked for a swing set, and knowing Joseph, she suspected he wouldn't long deny his son the chance for another skinned knee.

It was one of the things she most admired about Joseph. Instead of being the overprotective parent one would expect of a man in his circumstances, he seemed perfectly willing to let Joey be a typical little boy. Dirt and blood—in small amounts only—never seemed to faze him.

"Need some help?" she asked, refusing to admit that shouting through a hedge was an odd way to communicate. So far it had been working quite nicely.

There was silence, then a loud sigh, and a disgusted reply. "What I need is an extra pair of hands."

It was what she'd been waiting to hear. "I'll be right there." She dropped the rake and darted through her house, glad for the excuse to go see him.

Joseph watched her coming across his lawn, and at that moment, hated the damned red pole to the swing set he was holding in place. There were a lot of other things he would rather be doing with his hands than stuffing a bolt through a hole.

She was smiling, and the flash of her teeth made his belly ache. Wisps of that autumn-colored hair kept blowing across her eyes, and every time she reached up to brush it away from her face, the motion pulled her breasts up just enough to drive a man crazy. Her long legs were, as usual, bare. Her short cutoff jeans were soft and frayed, and they molded to her slender figure with every step she took. He groaned.

Molly heard the sound. She took the last few steps on the run, certain that he was in a terrible bind from the position he was in.

"I've got it," she said, sliding her own hands up beneath his, leaving him free to insert the bolt and put on the nut.

Her hands were slender. A small nick on her forefinger made him want to lean down and kiss away the pain, small though it might be. Reluctant to remove his hands and break their touch, he waited, and time ceased.

Molly looked up and was caught in a dark, impenetrable stare. She watched his eyes, and the way his gaze swept across her face, lingering longer than needed on her mouth, on her chin, on the way their bodies touched as she stood beside him.

She inhaled, then shuddered from an unexpected ache in a long-forgotten portion of her heart. It had been so long since she'd let herself care. Her gaze fixed as she counted four beads of sweat across his forehead and one in the center of his upper lip, and she wondered if he would put as much passion into making love as he did in making swing sets for his child.

Joseph watched the blue in her eyes turn gray and stormy, saw her body's reaction as her nipples hardened beneath her tank top, and knew that it wouldn't take much for their bodies to wind up tangled in the metal to which they were holding.

"Don't let go," he whispered softly.

She shook her head, unable to answer. *I would never let you go, Joseph Rossi. It's you who'd better hang on.*

❧ Four

Molly clipped the stem of the daisy in her hands to within a couple of inches of the bloom, inserted a thin, flexible piece of floral wire through it and then up through the blossom. Moving without conscious thought, she yanked a strip of white floral tape from the roll and began wrapping the wired stem. When she had finished, she laid it beside the others just like it on her work table that would soon become the elaborate bridal bouquet she was creating.

Wiping her hands on the seat of her pants to rid them of the sticky residue left from the floral tape, she began to assemble the bits of green fern and baby's breath that would form the halo of the bouquet. Anxious now that she'd actually begun to create the arrangement, the work went quickly.

Inserting, bending, and coaxing, she worked the flowers until they formed the perfect shape.

Cora poked her head around the display cooler. "Are you almost through? Harry has the palm fronds and archway already loaded." And then she grinned and lowered her voice so that the browsing customers could not overhear. "This wedding is going to look like it took place in a jungle. Did you ever see so much green stuff in your life?"

Molly nodded, absently listening to Cora's gossip, while most of her focus was on the work in her hands. But Cora wasn't exaggerating. The mother of the bride had literally bought out the store's supply of green and leafy plants as well as ordering a number of portable stands that would be filled at the church with layer upon layer of palm fronds.

"Just give me another second . . . there!" Molly stepped back to eye her project, then gave the last of the ribbon around the bouquet a fluff and straightened the lengths of lover's knots hanging below.

After spritzing the bouquet liberally with water, she slipped it into a large cellophane bag and handed it to Cora with a relieved flourish.

"I'm gone," Harry said as he collected the bride's bouquet from his wife and headed for the delivery van. "See you when I see you."

Several seconds of silence passed as Molly and Cora looked at each other and then unexpectedly burst into laughter.

"It's the same every time," Molly said. "First the euphoria of the order, then the mundane business of ordering the flowers from market. Next comes the day of decision. To create today . . . or wait till the last minute, take a chance on a slow day and work like hell. I always tell myself that next time I'll plan ahead, and next time never comes."

Cora nodded. "But you love it," she said.

Molly grinned. "I love it."

Cora began picking up bits and pieces of snipped ribbon and crushed leaf, then wiping and mopping around the work area while Molly headed for her office. Much as she hated to do it, it was almost the first of the month and time to do the billing.

She turned the corner in the hallway, her mind on the list of things to be done. The piece of palm frond came into her line of vision at the same time she stepped, but it was too late to stop the motion. Her foot connected with the wet leaf, and the next thing she knew she was flat on her back on the concrete floor, staring up at a brown water spot on the ceiling.

Oh, darn, the roof has a leak.

The thought was inane, but she had no intention of wondering why she'd chosen this particular moment to consider the issue of leaky roofs. She was just thankful she could still think, because she was afraid to move. The loud crack she'd heard when she hit the floor had come from something, and if her body was in pieces, she didn't want to know.

"Cora, do you think you could come here for a minute?" she called weakly.

Cora laid down her mop and started down the narrow hallway that led toward the back of the building when she saw Molly stretched out on the floor.

"Oh my God!" she shrieked. "Don't move. I'll call an ambulance!"

"No!" Molly groaned. "Just come help me up."

Cora was on the boundary between panic and tears when she knelt at Molly's side.

"Oh, honey, where does it hurt?" she asked.

Molly grinned slightly. "I'm afraid to find out. Let's try this one step at a time."

She wiggled a foot, and then the other. Nothing fell off. Nothing hurt—much. She lifted her arm, and then the other, then swept the disarray of curls from her face with shaky hands.

"So far, so good," she said. "Now help me, I'm going to try to sit up."

"Oooh, I don't know about this," Cora mumbled. "I still think we should call for help. What if you've hurt your back?"

"If I have, I'll know it in a minute," Molly said. She extended her arms and Cora pulled.

The effort took more out of Molly than she'd imagined. Pain shot through her back and then eased, rocketed through her head, and then subsided. She sat up, then flexed her knees and rested her head on them, unwilling, for the moment, to move any farther.

"Molly?"

She heard the fear in Cora's voice, but for the life of her, it was impossible to talk. If she opened her mouth, she would probably scream.

Minutes passed, and finally, when Molly could focus, with Cora's help, she stood upright.

"Good Lord," Molly said. "That was stupid."

"It was an accident," Cora corrected. "What made you fall?"

Molly pointed at the culprit still stuck on the bottom of her shoe. Cora frowned, bent down, and removed it before a repeat performance could occur.

"I'm calling Harry," Cora said. "You need to go to the emergency room and get yourself checked out."

"Don't be silly," Molly said. "He's in the middle of that wedding, remember? Besides, I just need to go home and get in a hot bath before everything stiffens up. I don't think anything's broken, but I know for darn sure that everything's bruised."

Cora wrung her hands, unwilling to let go of the idea of calling for help. "I hate this," she said. "I don't think you should be alone. What if you have a concussion? What if you've cracked a bone? You live alone, honey. Maybe you should come home with us."

Cora fussed absently with her short gray hair, worrying at the bit over her ear as she tucked it behind the earpiece of her eyeglasses. She couldn't bear the thought of Molly alone and in pain.

"No way," Molly said. "Besides, if I get in bed and can't get out, I'll call an ambulance myself. Remember, I have neighbors, good neighbors. If I need help, all I have to do is yell."

Cora hushed. She'd seen this look on Molly's face before and knew better than to argue.

"Oh, no!" She pointed to the crushed plastic on the floor. "Your new phone!"

Molly sighed with relief. Her compact portable phone, the one she'd stuffed in her hip pocket, was in pieces on the floor.

"Thank God that's what I heard break," she said. "I thought it was me."

Cora glared. "You need your head examined," she muttered.

Molly put a hand on either side of her own head, wiggled it gently back and forth, and tried to grin. "It feels all right."

"If you're making jokes, I suppose you can't be all that bad," Cora said. "But I swear, you're not driving yourself home. Either wait for Harry or call a cab."

"Yes, nurse." Molly hugged her to lighten the teasing remark she'd made. "Thanks for caring. Sometimes I don't know what I'd do without you and Harry. You've become as dear to me as my own parents were."

Cora tried to smile, but her chin wobbled instead. She was short and stocky, but when she had to, she could move like a skate bug on water, and she left on the run to call a cab.

Minutes later, Cora stood at the window, watching as the cab swung out into the city traffic, her eyes narrowing against the glare of the afternoon sun as she considered what she was about to do. Then she headed for Molly's office and began searching through her Rolodex. When she found the number she was looking for, she dialed. Her hands were shaking, but her voice was strong as she waited for someone to answer the phone.

"Red Earth Designs."

"Mr. Rossi, please," Cora said.

"He's with a client," the secretary told her. "If you'll leave your name and—"

"I'll hold," Cora said. "I think this is an emergency."

"Is this the day-care center?" Marjorie Weeks asked, suddenly aware of the implications the call could hold.

"No," Cora said, "I'm calling from the Garden of Eden."

Marjorie frowned. This didn't sound like that witch who'd been seeing her boss, but she didn't trust her not to try deception, just to bother him during business hours.

"I'll give him the message," Marjorie Weeks offered.

"I said I'll hold," Cora replied, and she did.

Minutes later, a man's deep voice came on the line, and when Cora was through talking, she hung up the phone in satisfaction. If that didn't send the cavalry—in the form of the new next-door neighbor—to Molly's rescue, nothing would. And while her conscience niggled at the meddling she'd just done, she kept telling herself that Molly would thank her for it later.

When the cab driver pulled up to Molly's front door, she got out with a groan, stumbling with every step as she let herself in. Without wasted motion, she headed for the bathroom, anxious to strip off her clothes and crawl into a hot bath, hoping it would stave off the stiffness creeping into her joints.

The tub filled swiftly, and as she stepped into the tub, she groaned. A long soak later, she groaned even louder when she tried to get out. To her horror, the harder she tried, the more painful and impossible it became. The water was tepid, her body felt like it was in traction, and moving was, at the moment, impossible. She looked at the clock on the vanity.

"No wonder I'm stiff," she muttered. "It's nearly three o'clock. I've been in the water for over an hour."

And from the way she felt, she'd be here a lot longer unless a miracle occurred. Not for the first time since she'd come home did she wish that she'd taken Cora's advice and gone on to the doctor. It felt like every bone in her body was bent, if not broken. She tested the faucets with her toes, trying unsuccessfully to turn on the hot water and warm up her bath. Then she used her feet to fiddle with the drain control in hopes of letting out the water. She finally gave up in defeat and moaned.

"I'm doomed. I need a miracle to get out of this

fix. I'll probably die from starvation, and when they find me dead, I'll be all waterlogged and pruney. I'll look like hell at my own funeral."

She was being dramatic and knew it, but laughing at herself was, at the moment, wasted effort. Instead, she gently eased her head against the edge of the tub and began wishing for that miracle.

Suddenly, the doorbell rang, and Molly jerked in reflex, sloshing water over the side of the tub and down onto the floor, soaking the bath mat, and sending shooting pains throughout her legs and arms.

"Oh God, that hurt," she groaned, as she tried unsuccessfully to get out of the tub. "That's just dandy—my miracle came without a front-door key."

For several more moments, the doorbell continued to ring, and just when Molly thought whoever it was had given up, a series of loud, persistent knocks could be heard. Once she thought she could even hear someone shouting, but she was too far in the back of the house to determine what was being said.

"I'm back here," she yelled. "Help! I need help!"

And then suddenly the shouts at the door ceased, and she closed her eyes and groaned, in certain despair that her miracle had given up and gone home.

But her fears were short-lived. Now she could hear footsteps of someone running around her house, and then the bellow of a familiar voice. She laughed aloud, then groaned when a sharp pain jabbed her from ear to ear, and she bit her lip to keep from laughing again. She'd heard that voice—and those very same colorful phrases—before. One of these days, when they got to know each other a lot better, she was going to mention his choice of language in times of stress.

"Joseph! I'm here," she called. "I can't get up."

The footsteps ceased, but the curses did not.

"There's an extra key beneath the azalea pot on the back porch," she yelled.

There was total silence, and then moments later she heard—along with another round of less-than-quiet curses—the lid of her barbecue grill hitting the concrete deck of her patio. She winced. She'd forgotten to mention the grill was not put away. By the time she was rescued, there might not be anything left of her house. He'd beaten her door, crushed her shrubbery, and probably broken her grill. If he didn't calm down, he'd probably break the key off in the lock and then she'd be in a fine fix.

Just about the time she heard the front door

open, then slam shut, it dawned on her that he'd gotten in. That was when she looked down and remembered that she was naked as the day she'd been born.

"Molly! Molly! Where are you?"

His voice was just below a roar. On the one hand, she'd never been so glad to hear a voice in her life. On the other, she was about to reveal all in a most unflattering manner.

Lord have mercy, she thought, then closed her eyes and swallowed. If she couldn't see Joseph, then it stood to reason he couldn't see her. Just as that thought sank in, Molly realized she'd probably hit her head a lot harder than she had first imagined. She wasn't making any sense at all.

"I'm in here," she said weakly.

He came through the door on the run with a worried expression on his face.

"Cora called. She said that you'd—"

The sentence hovered and died on his lips, right along with the last ounce of chivalry he'd been saving for damsels in distress. If he did what he should, he would already be backing out to give her the space she obviously needed, but something had happened to his feet. They didn't move any faster than his mouth, and he couldn't talk. He swallowed twice, took three deep breaths, and tried to remember his Boy Scout pledge, then he remembered he'd never been a Scout. Nothing came to mind but the pledge of allegiance to the flag, and he was pretty sure Molly didn't want to hear it.

He rolled his eyes, thrusting his chin in a stubborn, determined gesture, and headed for the tub.

I can do this . . . if I concentrate, he told himself. *Hell no!* he amended, as he knelt beside the tub and caught a watery glimpse of her body. *Concentration is the last damn thing I need right now.*

"Molly?"

She didn't answer, but her eyes squeezed shut a little bit tighter. He hid a grin, and then sighed as he began working her fingers loose from the sides of the tub. All of a sudden they came loose, and he threaded them through his hand and tried not to stare at her long-limbed beauty.

"Honey . . . are you all right? Cora said you fell."

She nodded, and he wasn't sure what answer he got. Either she was all right or it was a positive response to his statement about her fall. But when a tear slid from beneath one closed eyelid, he groaned. Oh God, she was going to cry! He fell apart when women cried.

"Now damn it, Molly, don't go and cry."

The warning took hold as she bit her lower lip and sniffed. Gently, he pulled a washcloth from the rack and swiped across her face in the same way he cleaned Joey's face during his bath. It was awkward but gentle, and got the job done. But as his fingers dipped into the water, he noticed how chilled her bath had become.

"Good grief, honey, the water's freezing. It's going to make you stiff."

"It already has," she said, and sniffed loudly.

Joseph reached over and pulled the plug. The water began to flow in a circular exit, lowering the level to reveal even more of her beauty.

Having convinced herself that she was somewhat concealed in the tub's depths, the sound of receding water made her suddenly panic.

"Don't look," she cried, while scarlet slashes of shame spread across her face and then downward.

He grinned. "Shoot, if that's all that's bothering you, it's too late. I already did."

Her eyes flew open. Her mouth dropped. And the dark lights dancing in his eyes told her more than he was able to say. He'd looked, and obviously liked what he saw. And he was still here, waiting for Molly to make the next move.

"You wretch," she moaned. "Then do the decent thing and hand me a towel."

Joseph grinned, then reached behind him, hand flailing blindly as he grabbed the first piece of terry cloth he touched. He handed it over with light aplomb.

"You call *this* a towel! Give me a break," Molly moaned.

Joseph looked down at the small hand towel he'd given her and tried not to laugh. It wouldn't have covered her face.

"It looks good to me," he said softly.

But this time he turned to see what he was grabbing, and lifted a huge bath towel from the vanity, then spread it over her like a sheet. She sighed with relief as the terry cloth touched her skin.

"Can you slide your arm around my neck, or does it hurt too much?" he asked. "If you want, I'll call an ambulance."

"Lord, no," she mumbled. "I'd like to think there were a few people left in town who haven't seen me in all my glory."

She was trying to make fun of her condition, but as far as he was concerned, she had understated the obvious. "Glory" didn't do her justice.

"Molly, look at me," he said, as he laid her gently down in the middle of her bed. She reluctantly complied. "I've seen naked women before."

"Not me," she said weakly, and turned away. "And if I'd wanted you to see me . . . like this . . . I didn't want it to be . . . like this."

He leaned down and kissed the top of her forehead, unable to resist the utter charm of her dismay. "I know," he said. "And frankly, I think this will ultimately cause me a lot more discomfort than it will you."

Her eyes flew open. She stared into his face, then her gaze slid down of its own accord and just as quickly flew back again.

"Oh!"

Joseph groaned. "You don't know the half. Now let's get sensible here. I'm calling a doctor. Either you go to him or he comes to you. What'll it be?"

Molly tried to move and then moaned. "There's a number by the phone. The doctor's an old friend. If he's not too rushed, I think he'll come out. Maybe you should call."

Joseph complied, and while they waited, he began drying her off. When he had finished, he dressed her as he would a baby, sliding a nightgown over her head and then gently straightening it beneath her until she was decently covered from neck to knee.

I will suffer for this tonight, he thought. But the thought wasn't enough to deter him from his mission. He would take this embarrassment away from her if it was the last thing he did today.

He'd often heard that from bad things, good

things grow. Well, Molly's fall had been bad, there was no denying that. But the few daydreams he'd allowed himself about his next-door neighbor had suddenly become insufficient. The wishes in his heart were now so much more. He could feel them sprouting all kinds of roots. Whether he liked it or not, whether he was ready to face another relationship or not, it had come to get him. Now all he had to do was get her well, and let nature take its course.

The silence between them was uncomfortable, as if each was trying to say something to ease the other's embarrassment, but couldn't think of what to say. Luckily, the doctor's arrival took away what was left of the strain. And while the doctor, who introduced himself as Dr. Marr, examined Molly, Joseph examined the pictures on the living room mantel, wishing that he and Joey had a perfect right to be among those Molly loved best.

Time passed, and he began to get nervous, keeping one eye on the clock and the other on the doctor, who was ending a speech about on-the-job accidents. He had less than fifteen minutes to go get Joey from day care. If nothing else happened, he'd just make it.

"I swear," Molly said. "I'll stay home from work the next two days. If I have any headaches, or unusual problems with my back, you'll be the first to know."

Dr. Marr nodded. He wasn't satisfied, but he couldn't force a patient to seek further treatment.

"Okay," he said. "But you've only yourself to blame if you've cracked a bone. I still wish you'd let me order a full set of X rays." But the determined look on Molly's face made him smile. "You're just like your mother, God rest her soul. If your father hadn't had such a fit, she'd have had you at home, instead of the hospital. What is it with you Eden women and hospitals, anyway?"

"I hate needles?"

"Bull," the doctor said. "You stick yourself twice as bad every day at that darn job of yours. Just look at the ends of your fingers. They're full of scratches and punctures from those fancy little doodads you use to keep flowers anchored in arrangements."

"Maybe I don't like all those soft-soled shoes you guys wear," Molly teased. "Makes a person nervous always being snuck up upon."

Dr. Marr's smile was gentle. He knew as well as Molly that her refusal to be admitted to a hospital was rooted in the fact that the last time she'd been in one, her world had come to an end. She'd lost the man she loved, the baby they'd made, and very nearly her sanity.

"I give up," Dr. Marr said. He turned his attention to Joseph. "If she has any real problems, I expect I'll hear from you."

Joseph nodded. "You can count on it. I don't want anything to happen to her." His dark eyes caught the wide-open stare in Molly's gaze before he turned away, unwilling for her to see more truth than tease in his statement. "She's the best neighbor I've had in years. Besides, she burns a damn good hot dog when she's pressed."

Dr. Marr laughed. "I sense a good story in that, however, I don't have enough time to hear it in the detail in which it deserves to be told. Save it for another day and another accident, okay?"

Molly groaned. "No more accidents for me, and thanks so much for coming, Dr. Marr. I knew I could count on you."

"I delivered you," he growled. "The least I can do is keep you alive long enough to come to my funeral. I expect flowers galore."

"You won't need flowers," Molly said. "I'll just chisel out a portion of the green around the ninth hole at Oak Tree. Enough to cover you and the casket should do it."

His smile was wide with delight. "Now you're talking," he crowed. "Keep in touch, girl. You're my kind of woman."

Joseph gaped. He couldn't believe it. These two

were talking about each other's demise in very lighthearted terms. He never considered that each of their respective jobs kept them in such close contact with mortality that they'd learned to accept it as a natural part of life. The doctor's life demanded that he do his best to heal, and when he failed, it was part of Molly's job to make the patient's final curtain call on earth a memorable one.

Joseph saw the doctor out and then stood quietly in the middle of Molly's living room, looking around at the world in which she lived.

It was full of family memorabilia, and for the first time, he realized that she'd probably grown up in this house. He thought he remembered her telling him that when her father remarried, he'd deeded the house to her. The walls were full of pictures of Molly in various stages of growing up. He shoved his hands in his pockets as he headed for her bedroom, suddenly aware of the vast differences in their respective childhoods.

Joseph had grown up in foster homes until his eighteenth birthday. Then he'd had a choice to continue in a downward spiral or change his life and crawl out of the black hole he called his world. He'd taken a step in the right direction and never looked back.

He sat down on the edge of her bed. "Are you

going to be all right alone? Do you need anything before I go? I'd stay longer, but I've got to go get Joey before they throw him out with the dishwater." He brushed a loose curl from her forehead and smiled to soften the blow of leaving.

"I'm fine," Molly said, and then winced. "At least, I will be in a few days."

As miserable as she was, she couldn't quit looking at Joseph—here, in her bedroom. The man seemed so out of place, and yet so at home, and she knew that if she didn't say something now, the next time they saw each other, she'd be too ill at ease to look him in the face.

"Joseph?"

"What, honey?" He stood, then leaned over her bed, intent on straightening her covers.

"I don't know how to thank you for what you did for me today," and then looked away, embarrassed all over again at the fact that he'd seen her naked.

The smile on his face died a slow, lingering death. He tried to think of a way to make light of the fact that he'd dried her like a baby, and couldn't think of anything except how soft her skin had felt beneath his fingers.

He paused in the act of smoothing the sheet. His fingers clenched. Slowly, he released the tight wad he'd made of the fabric and inhaled softly as he fell into the deep blue well of her gaze.

"I do," he said.

Molly was so tuned into his stare that she forgot what she'd said. "You do, what?" she mumbled, and watched his hands sliding up the sheet toward her face.

"Know how you can thank me," he whispered.

Her soft little gasp told him all he needed to know. He leaned closer, closer, until he could see himself reflected in the pupils of her eyes, and then her eyes closed and her mouth parted as she waited for him to come in.

It was an invitation he could not resist.

The tentative foray of his lips around her mouth was enough to make her shiver. Each touch became more than the last, yet not enough to assuage the increasing need she felt to take him, and his weight, into her. To cherish the feel of a man, her man, within her arms, inside her body, and know the fulfillment that can only come with loving.

But it was the thought of loving that made her panic, and it was enough to break their tenuous bond.

Joseph stared long and hard at the wild, almost frightened expression in those eyes. Watching her lips tremble, he knew that whatever ghosts had haunted her life were still in residence.

"I'm not going to apologize for the fact that I caught you with your guard—and your pants—down," he said, unable to resist the gentle thrust.

Molly's mouth formed a perfect O. He didn't give her time to decide whether it was from indignation or admiration. Before she knew it, he'd straightened, winked, and was gone, slamming the front door behind him.

She looked up at the ceiling, trying very, very hard not to grin, and lost the war with herself. She slid her fingers across her mouth, testing their texture, almost expecting them to have changed shape from the fire of his touch. But they were still there. Only one thing was different.

She couldn't seem to wipe the smile off her face.

"Oh, rats!" Molly watched helplessly as the orange she'd just dropped rolled beneath the kitchen table and out of her reach. As stiff and sore as she was, leaving it there was definitely an option to consider.

She was in the middle of a debate with herself about the wisdom of getting down on her hands and knees when the doorbell rang. She glanced at her watch, noting that it was nearly noon, and fully expected to see either Cora or Harry as she answered the door.

"Joseph!" She knew the expression on her face was silly. She could tell by the matching one on his own.

"I brought lunch." He waved a sack beneath her nose as he let himself inside.

"Good," she said, inhaling the tempting aroma of burgers and fries. "Today I can be easily had."

Joseph wiggled his eyebrows in a creditable imitation of Groucho Marx, unaware that his dimple completely neutralized any hint of lechery he might be trying to imply. "Exactly what can I have for a"—he set the sack on the kitchen table and peered inside—"cheeseburger and fries?"

"My undying gratitude," Molly said, "and a promise not to put out a contract on your life if you keep your mouth shut about yesterday."

The mention of yesterday and what had occurred sobered him instantly. The entire episode had kept Joseph up most of the night. But it wasn't from worry, it was from want. He'd been haunted by the fact that he'd held her naked in his arms, dried and dressed her as if she were a child, and tried to pretend it had all been done in the name of neighborly duties. The last damn thing he'd been feeling like when he'd left her alone was a Good Samaritan. He'd felt a whole lot more like an unsatisfied Peeping Tom.

"It's a deal," he said softly.

"I have one other request," Molly said, and unintentionally leaned toward him. "There's something I need from you."

Joseph caught his breath. Whatever was on her mind was all right with him.

"What is it, Molly?" he asked softly.

She pointed under the table with her toe. "Will you?"

"Will I what, honey?" he repeated, and traced the lower edge of her lip with his thumb as he imagined the effort it would take to crawl beneath that table with her. Imagining that it would be well worth the effort to try.

"Pick up my orange."

"Orange? You want me to pick up an orange?"

Molly grinned at the look of blank confusion on his face. "I dropped it just before you came. I was debating with myself about whether or not I could get up if I got down. I don't think I want to test the theory, especially since you've arrived. So . . ."

He knelt, crawled under the table, and retrieved the orange without further comment, handed it to her straight-faced, and asked, "Do you want ketchup on your fries?"

"Please."

The meal began and ended with the scent of orange permeating the air between them.

Joseph sighed, full of food and satisfied with the company as he wadded the wrapper from his burger and began collecting the rest of the refuse from the table. He could tell from watching Molly's face during their impromptu meal that moving was still very painful.

He leaned across the table and swiped at a bit of ketchup on the corner of her mouth with the edge of a napkin, then resisted the urge to sweep her into his arms.

"How do you feel today?"

She tilted her face, accepting his ministering touch as her due. "As Harry would say, sore as a boil. And I didn't sleep worth a darn last night."

Me either, Joseph thought. *But not for the same reasons.*

Silence hung heavily between them. His eyes were dark, the gaze intense. She stared down at his hands and for a moment, remembered how gently he'd lifted her from the tub. And then she looked back up at his face, centering on the curve of his mouth, and remembered the kiss they'd shared, and knew that it wasn't enough. She wanted more.

"Molly?"

The question was in his eyes as well as on his lips. She inhaled sharply, uncertain whether or not to voice what was in her heart, when the phone rang and interrupted the mood of the moment. It rang again, and then again, and finally Joseph moved.

"Eden residence," he said, then turned and handed Molly the phone. "It's Cora, for you."

From a distance, Joseph admired the competence with which Molly dealt with her business, and wished that he could deal with the feelings inside himself as easily. He wanted Molly Eden to look at him as more than a next-door neighbor. He also wanted her to see him as more than Joey's father. But Joseph didn't know if he was going to get what he wanted. Whether she knew it or not, their future was in Molly's hands.

When she had finished her conversation, he hung up the phone, then stuffed the trash into the garbage and washed and dried his hands without saying a word. Molly was the one to break the silence. And when she did, it was nothing more than a groan.

"Oohh." She tried to smile through pain as she pulled herself to her feet. "This will teach me to watch where I walk."

Joseph scooped her into his arms and then

stood in the middle of the kitchen floor, ignoring the look of shock on her face.

"Where do we go from here?" he asked. "To the living room, the backyard, or—"

"How about to bed," Molly said.

"Sounds good to me," Joseph whispered, and watched with delight at the way her cheeks turned pink.

"That's not what I meant, and you know it," she said.

He grinned. "I had a feeling I wasn't going to be included in this invitation. But . . . it never hurts to hope," he said.

Molly pointed toward the back of the house. "You know the way," she said. "Just drop me anywhere in the vicinity of the mattress. I'll take it from there."

Joseph carried her through the house without speaking, set her in the middle of her bed, and then leaned forward, piercing her with a stare that sent shivers of excitement and promise threading through her system.

"Lady, this is the last time I put you in bed alone," he said softly. "Next time I have no intentions of leaving. You'd do well to remember that, okay?"

She shuddered, swallowed a lump in her

throat, and nodded. There was little left to say. And moments later, she heard the front door slam. She was left with nothing but the memory of his warning and the look on his face when he'd told her good-bye.

❧ Five

For once, the day-care center was quiet, but only because the children were outside on the playground. Even then, Lila Forshee could hear a subdued version of their squeals and shrieks as they played.

Out of habit, she went to the window, just to make sure that the noises she was hearing were those of delight. The children were everywhere, flitting from swing to slide and back again like tiny windup dolls. For a moment, she just watched, thankful for having a job she loved so much, and then suddenly frowned as she noticed the change in the sky.

When the children had gone out to play, it had been the white-hot blue of an Oklahoma summer day. Now it was shaded in dark, somber colors and overcast with a skirt of boiling clouds. From their appearance, the low overhang of dark gray clouds could unload their moisture at any minute.

She spun from the window and switched on her radio, quickly tuning it to a weather station. As she'd suspected, storm warnings were in the area. It was past time to get the children inside, although she knew they were going to object. Playtime at the center was their favorite time of the day.

As she ran outside to call them in, she heard the first of a series of low, angry rumbles from the overhead clouds.

"Bring the children inside immediately," she called. "We're under a storm warning."

In the beginning, the children's objections were loud, but they didn't last long. When the first drops of rain began to fall, they scrambled off of the playground equipment without any fuss and made a dash for the door like a covey of little quail heading for the protection of their mother's wing.

Lila grinned at their shrieks of delight as the raindrops began to land on their heads and faces. She stood in the doorway, holding the door ajar as the kids and the helpers scrambled inside; she shouted another encouragement to the group in the farthest corner of the playground, urging them to hurry as well, because the storm was nearly upon them. But no sooner had she called than she realized the panic on the playground had put one of the children in danger.

"Oh, no!"

Lila started out the door, aware that no matter how fast she ran, she would not get to the child in time to stop his fall. "Tracy! Stop the child on the slide!"

Her shout got the attention of one of her helpers who was herding the remaining children toward the door. The assistant reacted in much the same manner as Lila had done. But they could already tell that they would not be in time to stop the fall. The child was already on an ill-fated move.

Joey had been frightened by the wind. And when the children's giggles and shrieks increased to fever pitch as the first drops of rain fell upon them, he panicked. Sliding down the slide would have been faster and simpler. But he was far too young to reason. Instinct sent him back the way he'd come. He was struggling to retrace his steps back down the ladder when he caught his toe.

For a long moment, he teetered on the edge, trying desperately to catch himself. But his arms were too short, and his strength not enough to stop the sway of his body. He fell through the air without making a sound, leaving them all with the last impression of his outstretched arms and the look of disbelief upon his face.

And then he hit the ground.

Lila cried out, then fear lent speed to her steps. It seemed to take forever, but it was in fact only seconds before she reached his side.

"Call 911," she shouted as she leaned over the child and began tracing his tiny body for obvious signs of broken bones.

The young assistant raced toward the office as Lila knelt in the rain-splattered yard beside the child. Touching his forehead, she winced at the flow of blood welling from a cut at his hairline, as well as the awkward angle at which he was lying. He looked like a little broken doll.

Lila was afraid to pick him up. "Joey, darling . . . where do you hurt?"

The child moaned, then slowly, and to her immense relief, opened his eyes and looked up. His expression was dazed, his eyes full of pain and of shock as he crawled out of the dirt and into Lila's lap. While she was happy that he had moved of his own volition, she was not surprised when he suddenly burst into tears.

"Want my Daddy," he cried, and then stuck his thumb into his mouth and began to sob.

She lifted him into her arms and made it inside

the office just as the deluge unloaded. Rain came down in blinding sheets, but Lila didn't notice. She was too busy trying to stem the flow of blood running down the child's face.

"Bring me some ice," she yelled as she ran to the washroom, "and call Joseph Rossi's office. Tell him to meet us at Saint Anthony's emergency room. And get the rest of the children out of here. The last thing I need is for all of them to go into hysterics."

Within minutes, an ambulance had arrived, and a paramedic began his examination of Joey while questioning Lila about the accident.

"I didn't want to move him after he fell," she said, "but he moved himself and crawled into my lap. That was when we came inside and called you."

The medic nodded. "Children are very resilient," he said. "I've seen kids fall from second-story windows and wind up with nothing more serious than a black eye." His tone lowered and the seriousness of Joey's possible injuries made them all take notice. "I've also seen them die from nothing more than a fall off a bed." Then he added. "Who's responsible for this child?"

Lila answered. "I am. I'm legally allowed to have first aid rendered to any of the children here.

But his father's office is near. I've instructed him to meet us at the hospital."

And then Tracy came running back into the room where Joey was being examined.

"Mrs. Forshee, Mr. Rossi's secretary is unable to reach him! She said he went out on a job site and didn't take his pager. She has no way of contacting him until he calls in."

Lila groaned as the paramedics began rolling Joey toward the waiting ambulance, and then she remembered.

"Call Molly Eden. Her name and number are on Joey's records. Tell her to meet us at Saint Anthony's and then keep calling Mr. Rossi's office. Do you hear me?"

Tracy nodded as the doors closed behind the child who was being wheeled away to the waiting ambulance.

Molly wiped her hands and then stretched her aching back. Sometimes standing was as tiresome as running a mile, and she'd been filling orders all afternoon.

Harry, if you've got the last of the flowers in water, would you mind holding down the fort for a while? I think I'll take an early afternoon and go by the flower market. I got a call from the rep earlier. There's a new shipment of pottery in the warehouse and we're nearly out."

Harry nodded, but felt compelled to add, "No problem, but do you really think you should go out? That storm cloud looks pretty fierce."

She looked out the window and shrugged. "Did Gary England say it was a tornado watch, or a tornado warning?"

Harry grinned. No self-respecting citizen of Oklahoma got nervous until their premier weatherman told them it was time to panic. "Just a watch," he answered.

"Then I'm gone," she said. "This time of year, every other cloud in the state is a storm watch. I don't worry until they update them to warnings."

"Spoken like a true Okie," Harry said.

The phone rang, breaking the mood of the moment, and Harry picked it up on the third ring.

"Garden of Eden," he said, and then frowned. "Molly, it's for you. Sounds serious—it's someone from your neighbor's day-care center."

Molly's heart thumped twice in rapid succession as she hurried to answer the phone. It had been nearly a week since the kiss and what she laughingly called her "fall from lack of grace." And in that time, she'd been wooed by the best. There were blue crayon pictures from Joey that she'd hung with pride on her refrigerator door and a goodly number of heart-stopping kisses that Joseph Rossi had stolen without asking. Although, to be fair, not once had Molly objected to the thefts.

"This is Molly Eden." Her smile disappeared. She paled, then turned a lighter shade of pale as she listened. "I'll be right there. In the meantime, keep trying his office."

She slammed down the phone, her hands trembling as she struggled to write down a set of instructions for Harry to relay to Joseph should he call here instead of the center, and then made a run for her jacket and purse.

"What?" Harry asked. "Is it bad news?"

She shook her head. "It sounds like it. All they said was Joey fell," she said. "But the ambulance is already on the way to Saint Anthony's with him, and they can't locate Joseph. I have to go."

"Call me," Harry said, then frowned as the raindrops outside turned into a wall of blowing water. "And for God's sake, drive carefully," he ordered.

And then she was gone, and Harry stared blindly at the rain and the wind, and knew that the storm outside was nothing to the one inside Molly Eden's heart. Whether she realized it or not, her reaction to this news had given her away.

Her relationship with Joseph Rossi had obviously gone way past neighborly.

Marjorie Weeks was in a panic. Joseph's pager was on the desk in his office. Because of that, she had no way to contact him and inform him of his son's accident, nor did she imagine, from the looks of the weather outside, that he'd be calling in any time soon. He hadn't answered his car phone, he didn't have the pager, she didn't know what to do.

She paced the floor, trying to think of an alternative plan, when the second phone call came from the center informing her that Molly Eden had been located and was en route to the hospital.

She made note of the information, fuming as she did that it wasn't decent for a child to be in the care of a woman like that. Memories of the first time they'd met, and of Molly Eden's teasing remark about not recognizing Joseph with his clothes on, disgusted her.

"It's just not right," Marjorie muttered. "A child needs his own mother. Not an overavailable female who happens to live next door."

She didn't see it as wrong that she was taking too much upon herself to worry about her boss's private life. As far as she was concerned, it was her duty to see that a nice man like Joseph Rossi didn't make the same awful mistakes as her ex-husband had done. It was that irrational thinking that made her do something very unlike her—something very unprofessional. She went into Joseph's office and snooped.

Days earlier, Joseph had remarked about needing to return certain papers to his safe-deposit box. She knew for a fact that they were papers that concerned his legal relationship with his son. After the incident at the day-care center, he'd had to show proof of his legal custody and guardianship rights as well as prove that he was really Joey's father. If she was right, the mother's name should be mentioned somewhere on the papers.

Her hands shook and her heart was pounding as she opened the file. Nervously, she glanced toward the closed door, then began to search. She didn't have long to look.

Shock at what she read overwhelmed her. Somehow, Joseph had coerced Joey's natural mother into giving up all rights and claims to her child forever. She was appalled at the clinical manner with which her rights had been disposed of. While Marjorie knew and accepted that many women could give birth and then give their child away, she wouldn't let herself believe that this was the case. In her mind, she was certain that if

Joey Rossi's mother knew what danger her child was in, she'd surely come running.

She wrote down the information she needed, and quickly returned the papers to Joseph's desk drawer. What he didn't know wouldn't hurt him, and, she thought, in the long run, he'd thank her. It was with that misguided bit of information and thinking that she went about doing her bit toward trying to ruin the rest of Joseph's life.

The windshield wipers gave a halfhearted swipe at the sheet of rain blowing against the windshield. But Molly knew the city like the back of her hand, and she negotiated the streets almost on autopilot. Instead, her thoughts were focused on the way Joey's arms felt as he threw them around her neck or the way that his eyes could well with unshed tears when his feelings had been hurt. She couldn't imagine him in pain. And she knew that when Joseph was finally found, he would be devastated, knowing that his baby had suffered alone. All she could do was get there as quickly and safely as possible. If Joey needed someone and his daddy wasn't available, then "momma" would have to do.

Her hands were shaking as she wheeled into the parking garage across the street from Saint Anthony's Hospital. Seconds later, she was out of her car and running before she remembered that she hadn't even put on her jacket. But there was no way she'd turn back. All she could think about was getting inside and looking into Joey's face, assuring herself that he was all right. He just had to be.

"God help me, I can't lose another child," she whispered, and then dashed out into the rain and across the street.

It didn't dawn on her that Joey wasn't hers to lose. He and his father had already taken up residence in her heart.

Lila Forshee was trying not to get hysterical. But the doctor and nurses who were tending Joey were having a difficult time keeping him still long enough for treatment. His screams and shrieks could be heard all the way down the long hallway in X-ray.

Joey Rossi's world was coming apart at the seams. Strangers were hurting him, and the unfamiliar smells and noises only added to his terror.

Lila paced the waiting area outside of the ER, hoping that someone would arrive soon who could soothe the child's fears. Her heart was breaking for the toddler in panic, but she'd been unable to calm him, and only wound up getting in the doctor's way. Waiting out here while he was being treated was her only option. She glanced at her watch, wishing as she had for the last few minutes that Joseph Rossi would make a miraculous appearance, and then she heard the rapid sound of footsteps and looked up. Relief came with the tall slender woman who was running in an all-out sprint down the hallway.

"Molly . . . thank God you're here!"

Lila's worried expression turned Molly's stomach. The room tilted. She refused to admit, even to herself, that she was scared out of her mind. Fainting was not an option. She grabbed Lila's arms, literally shaking the answer out of her.

"Where is he? Is he hurt badly? I could hear him screaming before I got off the elevator."

Lila pointed, and Molly ran.

"Momma!"

The child's kicking and screaming stopped simultaneously with Molly's arrival. His silence shocked the doctor and nurses in attendance almost as much as what he said. They turned as one in time to see the slender woman who burst through the doorway. They didn't even have time to move before she rushed past them, grabbed Joey from the bed and clasped him to her breast as if she needed him to take her next breath.

Tears that Molly had been willing away suddenly flowed. But it didn't matter now. She was here, and Joey was in her arms.

"Well now, little man," the doctor said, as he leaned against a cabinet and smiled at the now near-silent child. "I see why you were so worried. I would be worried too, if I didn't have someone this pretty holding me."

Molly smiled through tears as she raked her gaze across Joey's face and body, trying not to gasp at the amount of blood on his clothes, then sank onto the bed with Joey cradled against her breast. She smoothed the hair away from his forehead, noting for the first time the three tiny stitches just below his hairline, and tried not to burst into a fresh set of tears. Joey'd had a big enough fit alone, he didn't need to see her distress and start a new one.

"How is he?" Molly asked, and unconsciously rocked Joey as he slipped his thumb into his mouth and tried to work himself up into another set of tears. His sniffles and sobs nearly broke her heart.

"Except for a cut on his forehead, which we managed to stitch—against his wishes, I might add—he seems to be fine. He's been x-rayed and given a thumbs-up, although I will say that Frank down in radiology will never be the same." The doctor grinned to make his point. "Sounds really echo down there. You could hear this fellow on the next floor." He pointed to the child in Molly's arms.

"I fell," Joey announced. "Want my daddy." Just thinking about his absent parent sent a fresh set of tears flowing, but the screams and shrieks had disappeared with Molly's arrival.

"I know, darling," Molly said, and hugged him gently, afraid to squeeze too hard and injure something bruised. "Daddy will be here as soon as Mrs. Weeks can find him, okay?"

Joey nodded, and snuggled against Molly's breast. "My momma," he said, clutched a handful of her shirt, and closed his eyes.

The doctor slid a practiced hand along the child's arm and let it slide gently across his wrist, pausing long enough to test the pulse rate of the child in Molly's arms.

"He should sleep," the doctor said. "We'd given him something for pain just before you arrived. He has no signs of concussion, no broken bones, only the cut on his forehead. But I recommend that you or your husband take Joey in to his pediatrician tomorrow morning and let him check him again, just to be safe."

Molly nodded. There was no use trying to explain to this man that she had no husband and no legal right to be holding this child. There was no way she was about to let go of Joey. And from the way Joey was holding onto her wet clothing, he had no intentions of letting go of her, either, even in sleep.

"What should I do?" Molly asked, aware that the feelings swamping her amounted to a lot more than overwhelming love for the child in her arms. "What if he wakes up in pain? Can he get his stitches wet? Will the medicine you gave him make him nauseous? Can I—"

The doctor smiled. "Spoken like a true mother. The nurse will give you a set of instructions. Other than that, use your instincts, and"—he put a gentle hand on Molly's shoulder—"when you get home, get into something dry so you don't get sick, too."

Molly shuddered and sighed. "Yes, Doctor." She shifted Joey's limp body in her arms to get a firmer grip, then walked out of the ER, pausing long enough to stuff the sheet of paper the nurse handed her into her hip pocket.

"I'll get a wheelchair," the nurse said.

"I don't need one," Molly said. "I'm not hurt, and I'm not putting him down. I'll carry him."

The nurse frowned, and then relented as she saw the doctor nod his approval from behind Molly's back.

"Is he all right?" Lila asked, as Molly walked out with the child in her arms.

Molly nodded. "Just a cut. He has stitches." Her mouth wobbled. "His first."

Lila sighed. "And from the looks of this little man, they won't be his last. He's one of the more daring children I have at the center."

"Just like his father," Molly said. "He dares a lot, too."

She couldn't help but remember her rescue from the bathtub and the unabashed way in which Joseph went about it.

"Did you drive?" Lila asked.

Molly nodded. "I'm across the street in the parking garage."

"We'll take the underground tunnel to get back to the parking garage. It'll save getting wet again, and I'll drive while you hold him. After I get you home, I'll call a cab."

"Thanks," Molly said. "I appreciate it."

Lila grinned wryly. "Don't thank me. I don't know what I'd have done if you hadn't showed up."

Molly looked down at the sleeping child in her arms, and resisted the urge to cry again. Her world had been rocked off its axis in a big way this afternoon. She wasn't certain what it all meant, but she had a feeling that things would never again be quite the same.

All the way across town, Molly clutched Joey

tight against her breast and prayed that Joseph would somehow be waiting when they arrived. When they turned the corner and started down the street, her heart dropped. His car was nowhere in sight.

"I have a key to Joseph's house," she said. "Just park in his driveway. You can call a cab from here. I don't want to put Joey to bed at my house and then have Joseph have to move him again later."

"Good idea," Lila said, and then she cocked her eyebrow as she parked Molly's car. "So . . . you have a key to his place, do you?"

Molly flushed, and stared down at the sleeping child in her arms. "It's not like you think. We're just friends."

Lila nodded sagely. "It's always good to have friends."

"You have my permission to shut up at any time," Molly said. "I can read your mind, and it's crawling in the gutter."

Lila wiggled her eyebrows. "There are worse places to be," she teased.

Molly looked up at the sky, thankful that there seemed to be an intermittent break in the rain. "Not today," she said. "If I don't miss my guess, the gutters—and the streets—will flood before this is over."

Lila made a run for the house, opened the door,

then stepped aside as Molly hurried in with Joey, who was still asleep in her arms. The only reaction he made to being moved or disturbed was to tug harder at the thumb stuck inside his mouth.

And then Lila was gone, leaving Molly alone in Joseph's house with Joey clinging tightly to her blouse. She walked to his bedroom, thinking she would put him down in his own bed. But each time she tried to lay him down, he would whimper and cry.

"Okay, baby," she whispered, and feathered a gentle kiss across his forehead. "We'll do it your way."

She headed across the hall into Joseph's room, trying not to think of what she was about to do. Careful not to disturb Joey's restless sleep, she kicked off her shoes, crawled across Joseph's bed on her knees, and when she was in the middle of the king-size mattress, stretched out with Joey still clinging fast to the front of her blouse, and lay down with the child still clutched in her arms.

Joey shifted, aligning himself beside her while refusing to give up the portion of Molly's shirt he held tightly in his fist. He whimpered once from remembered pain and sucked once or twice on his thumb before his lips went slack.

Molly smiled. She could see the tiny tongue work occasionally against Joey's thumb, and managed to kiss the top of his head without disturbing him. They were both filthy and wet, but moving or changing clothes at this time was not an option.

Joey's breathing eased, his restlessness ceased, and before long, he and Molly were fast asleep in the middle of Joseph's bed.

The storm was moving in quickly. The contractor was shouting orders to the carpenters and the electricians to stop all work until the wind and rain had passed. Lightning was a hazard on a construction job, and he had no intentions of endangering his men.

"You'd better get out of here while you can," he told Joseph, pointing to all the dry, barren land on which the new building was being erected. "If we get much rain, this place will look like a mud bog. I don't think that low-slung car of yours will go far in three or four feet of goop."

Joseph nodded. "We've about got all the kinks worked out of this latest problem, anyway," he said. "If the owner comes up with any more good ideas, let me know. We'll see what we can do to head him off."

The contractor grinned. He liked working with this laid-back man from the Deep South. Most architects would have been throwing a righteous fit at the thought of someone changing their drawings on a whim, which is what the owner had tried to do. It hadn't dawned on the owner that the wall he'd wanted to eliminate was there for a reason. It had taken Joseph and the contractor the better part of an hour to point out that if the wall went, the west roof probably would go next of its own accord.

Stress factors and building codes were not in the owner's vocabulary. He wanted wide, open spaces. They compromised and settled on faux marble columns instead of the solid wall. The structure would still have the support it needed and the owner would have the feeling of open space between the columns.

"Met the owner's missus yet?" the contractor asked.

Joseph shook his head.

"Just wait," the contractor promised. "Her favorite color is purple."

Joseph rolled his eyes and laughed. "Thank God I'm only the architect, not the interior decorator."

He headed for his car and had just pulled onto pavement when the downpour hit. Because of the rain, traffic was heavy and slow. It took him longer than normal to get back into town, and for some reason, the longer he drove, the more uneasy he became. He glanced at his watch, noting the time, and decided to swing by the office before going to day care to pick up Joey. It was only after he'd parked in the lot that he noticed his car phone was off.

For a moment, nerves skittered, and then he shrugged. Becoming a parent was making a real worrywart out of him, and he grinned at the thought of Joey. His son was a constant joy.

"Oh, Mr. Rossi!" Marjorie Weeks burst into tears as Joseph entered the office. "I called and called. But you left your beeper here, and your car phone doesn't work."

Joseph felt sick. His instincts hadn't been wrong after all. "What happened?" he asked.

"The day-care center called. Joey fell. They took him to Saint Anthony's and then . . ."

Joseph was gone. The door slammed shut behind him, but Marjorie could still hear the sounds of his footsteps running down the hall.

It took one phone call to the day-care center during the drive to the hospital to learn that his son had already been released. When Lila Forshee calmly explained that she'd called Molly when she couldn't reach him, a feeling of overwhelming relief made him shake. What would he have done without her? He made a quick adjustment in direction and headed toward home as he continued to grill Lila on Joey's condition.

"Is he all right?" Joseph asked, needing to know, yet afraid of the answer.

"Yes," Lila said. "I'm so sorry he got hurt. He fell off the slide. I saw it happening, but couldn't get there in time to catch him."

Joseph muttered under his breath as he switched lanes of traffic, trying not to curse in Lila's ear at the stupidity of the driver he'd just passed.

"I'm the first to admit that things can happen so quickly you don't even see them coming." He could still remember his shock and fear the day Joey had wandered out of the house and his relief upon learning that Molly had found him.

"What were his injuries?" Joseph asked as guilt and dismay overwhelmed him. His son had been hurt and he'd had to make his first trip to a hospital without his daddy.

"He has three stitches. Nothing else seems to have been injured, although Molly did tell me that the doctor suggested you take Joey to his pediatrician tomorrow for a thorough checkup."

Joseph nodded. "I'll be in touch," he said shortly, and hung up his car phone. He turned swiftly off of Sixty-third Street, anxious to get home.

When he turned into his driveway, he came to a stop only inches from the bumper of Molly's car, then hit the ground running.

The house was quiet, too quiet. He ran through the rooms with his belly churning. Although every instinct he had made him want to shout his arrival, the same instinct told him not to make a sound.

And then he started down the hall toward his son's room, expecting to see Molly sitting beside Joey's bed or holding him in her arms. But the door to his room was ajar, and when he looked inside, it was obvious he had to look no farther. They were sound asleep, wrapped in each other's arms in the middle of his bed.

He froze on sight, inhaled sharply at the picture, and tried not to cry. But tears came anyway, and they were healing tears of relief.

Moving silently, he hurried into the room and then stood beside the bed, unable to do more than just look. The sight of drying blood on his son's clothes made him sick, as did the small white bandage on Joey's forehead. He saw tear tracks on the child's face and he saw much, much more. He saw the way Joey was clutching at Molly's shirt as if he'd never let go. And he saw the way Molly had cradled the toddler against her body, protecting him, even in her sleep.

He knelt, tracing a finger along the edge of Joey's hair, lifting it just enough to see the first edge of stitches beneath the bandage. His hand shook, as did his breath.

Molly opened her eyes but didn't move. Looking into Joseph's pain, she smiled softly and then shook her head in answer to the unspoken question she could see on his face.

"He's okay," she said. "The doctor said so. I'm sorry we messed up your bed. He wouldn't turn me loose."

"Hell, I don't blame him."

Joseph's voice was low, barely above a whisper, but Molly heard him just the same. She tried to move, but Joey's hand clenched the fistful of her shirt that much tighter.

"Here, let me," Joseph said, and began to unwind his son's hand from Molly's clothing.

His knuckles brushed the underside of her breast more than once as he worked, and more than once, he leaned so close she imagined she heard his heart beat. Molly tried to ignore the increase of her own heartbeat, as well as the muscle that jerked in Joseph's cheek. But it was no use. He was too close and too much man to ignore.

Joey moaned in his sleep, and then whimpered as Joseph lifted him out of Molly's arms.

"I'll be right back," he said, and gently kissed his child's forehead as he carried him from the room.

"Daddy?" Joey muttered, somehow aware that his world was back in order.

"Daddy's right here," Joseph said. "I'm going to lay you down in your little bed, okay? Right next to Thumper."

Joey sniffed, sucked, and pulled his stuffed rabbit beneath his belly as his father laid him down.

It didn't take Joseph long to remove Joey's shoes and cover him lightly with a blanket. For a long, long moment, he stood over his son's bed and stared, thinking that no matter how fiercely one loved, it did not protect those in question from harm.

He swallowed harshly, unwilling to admit, even to himself, how panicked he'd been, or how thankful he was that Molly was in their lives. In that instant, he realized that he'd done something he swore he'd never do again. He'd become dependent on a woman. He didn't know whether to curse himself or thank God that he was beginning to heal.

Satisfied that his son had survived the incident just fine without him, he gave him a last, lingering look, lightly touched his forehead, and then walked out of the room, shutting the door just enough to keep out any sudden noises.

When he walked back across the hall, Molly was gone. Frowning, he pivoted and hurried toward the living room.

He caught her at the front door. "Molly . . . sweetheart . . . where are you going?"

The hurt in his eyes made her sorry, but she'd been too aware of what he'd been thinking when she'd awakened to see him at the side of the bed, touching first his son, and then her, all the while blinking back tears. The accident had amplified the feelings simmering between them.

She shrugged, and tried to smile. "I'm wet, and you're here. You don't need me anymore."

"No!" He pulled her into a rough, shaky embrace. "That's where you're wrong, Molly. I *do* need you. You'll never know how much." He felt her struggle briefly within his arms, and held her a little tighter. "Don't turn away from me," he begged. "You hold my son . . . why in God's name won't you hold me?"

The pain in his voice was her undoing. She ceased her struggles, then sighed in defeat. And when he wrapped his arms around her waist, she tilted her chin and stared him straight in the face.

"Because I'm afraid you'll let me go," she said softly.

Joseph forgot to breathe. There was so much old pain in what she'd admitted that he feared anything he said would be wrong.

"Willingly? . . . Never," he said.

As his hands slid down her back, pulling her hips tighter against him, moving them together to test for fit, she shuddered. The fit was perfect.

"Molly?" The question was there, awaiting her answer.

"I'm awfully wet," she warned.

"Then take off your clothes."

✑ Six

Molly held her breath. There was more than need in Joseph Rossi's eyes. She saw trust, and promises—and she saw love. It was—for her—enough.

"I don't think I can," she said. "I'm shaking."

"God help me, so am I," Joseph said, and lifted her off her feet, urging her closer until she could do nothing but hold on.

With nothing but the wall at her back to hold her up, Molly gave herself to the man in her arms, allowing her body to grow accustomed to the changing shape of his. Her legs trembled, but her heart was strong. She wanted to belong to this man more than she'd wanted anything in her life.

His mouth slid across her neck and then up, sampling the texture of her skin and lips with gentle but increasing pressure. And then he fitted his mouth to hers with perfect precision and took what she offered. Breath shortened, lungs ached, hands shook, and need grew.

"Molly . . ." The tortured whisper came quickly as he pressed himself harder against the cradle of her body.

She gasped as his hands slid down between them, cupping her and then moving in a gentle, persuasive motion. And when he set her back on her feet and then cupped her hips, pulling her closer to him, she begged for more. Willingly, he complied as his body replaced his hands. She moved closer, trying to pull him into the pain he'd created.

"Oh Molly," Joseph whispered. "I need to get you into my bed. I don't think I can wait much . . ."

"Don't," she begged.

Time ceased. Joseph could hardly think. She'd asked something of him that was going to prove damn near impossible, if not fatal.

"You want me to stop?" he asked, trying to separate what was on her face from what she'd said.

"No! No!" she begged. "I don't want you to wait. Please," she said, and slid her hands beneath his shirt, lifting it up and off without disturbing a button.

"Aaahh."

It was all he could say as her nails raked lightly across the breadth of his chest and then around, digging into the tightened muscles under his shoulder blades.

Blindly, without thought or caution, his hands moved of their own accord. Clothing shifted, then dropped to the floor, hearts stopped, and then jump-started again with the first touch of skin against skin.

"Like this, baby," he whispered, and shifted her legs to allow him access to her body. He shivered as his hands slid over the satiny surface of her skin, and when he felt the heat, he moved and made them one.

Molly was instantly lost in eyes so dark that she couldn't see past the passion. And when he lifted her up, and then let her back down, her breath thickened as their bodies merged. As he shut his eyes in momentary ecstasy, he groaned against her ear, and she forgot what she'd been about to say.

At first, there was only the feeling of being made whole, of being complete when, for so long, she'd known that there was a part of her missing. And then other, more subtle sensations began to take hold. The strong, constant ebb and flow of their bodies moving against and then with each other, the way the muscles across his back bunched beneath her hands as the tension stretched between them.

Joseph couldn't think. There was nothing in his life at this moment except the feel of this woman in his arms. The way her body softened and warmed, accepting him into herself without caution. He shook, wondering—praying—that his legs would not give way and tumble them both into the floor. It had been so long, and it felt so good.

And he began to move faster, in and out, over and over, until her breathing changed and he felt her tightening around him. Molly shook, whispering soft, almost nonexistent promises against his cheek, begging him to finish what they'd both begun.

"Oh God," he groaned, and slid his hands behind her hips to cushion them from the wall as he moved deeper. It was time.

Heat spiraled, breath melded, and Joseph covered her lips with his own. And when she arched against the final thrust of his body and then collapsed within his arms, he swallowed her sigh, and knew a pleasure unlike anything he'd ever experienced.

Spent passion left them weak and shaking, helpless and unwilling to move.

Her name was a prayer upon his lips. "Molly, Molly," he whispered, raining kisses over and over across her face and neck as he searched her body, gently assuring himself that what they'd given to each other had been willingly received. "Tell me you're . . . tell me that I didn't . . ." He shuddered, and leaned his forehead against hers, unable to finish what he'd been trying to say.

"I am. You didn't."

She sighed as she felt him move. Once again she was Molly. Alone, but no longer empty. He'd done what she'd thought no one could ever do again. He'd filled her soul.

"Don't be sorry that happened," he begged, and cupped her face in his hands.

"Only if it never happens again," she said, smiling through tears as she rearranged her clothing.

Joseph stared, forgot what he'd been about to say, and began to grin.

"I have a request," he asked, threading his fingers through the tousled abandon he'd made of her curls.

She looked up and waited. Right now, she'd have refused him nothing.

"When we do this again . . . can we do it lying down? My legs are still shaking." He waited for an answer. "So, what do you say?"

"My clothes are still wet," Molly said, and cocked an eyebrow upward in a teasing fashion.

"God help me," Joseph said, and scooped her into his arms.

"Wait," Molly said, just as he started into his room with her in his arms. "Put me down."

Joseph did as he was asked, expecting everything except what she did next.

Molly slid to the floor, gave him a gentle pat on the cheek to remember her by, and tiptoed across the hall, peeking quietly through the half-open door of Joey's room. Shuddering, she leaned her head against the door frame, watching Joey as he slept.

"I've never been so scared," she said, as she felt Joseph's arms sliding around her from behind. "I could hear him screaming when I got off the elevator. I ran and I ran until I thought my heart would burst."

Joseph was too full of emotion to speak. He was hearing—from a woman who needn't have cared—what he'd longed to hear from Joey's real mother: concern, compassion, and a nurturing responsibility that only comes through love.

"My heart's about to burst, too," he whispered. "But for an entirely different reason." He turned her within his embrace. "I don't know whether you're ready to hear this or not, but I need to say

140

it before we make love again." He cradled her face in his hands, gently rubbing his thumbs across her lower lip to keep it from trembling, and then sighed, leaned down, and they touched, cheek to cheek.

"What is it, Joseph? You can tell me anything. If you're afraid I'm going to pressure you into some commitment, or some declaration, don't be. What I feel for you . . . what happened between us . . . does not encompass rules."

He shook his head, and allowed himself a lingering taste of her lips before he spoke.

"But I do. I have rules. I can't make love to you again, until I tell you . . ." He shuddered as his arms slipped around her, afraid to look into her face as he spoke the words. "I love you, Molly Eden. And as God is my witness, I can't face the thought of you not loving me back."

Molly's heart jumped within her breast. The small cry of joy was all she allowed herself, and then she was in his arms.

"Take me to bed, Joseph," she said, whispering softly against his ear. "And quit worrying . . . love comes easy . . . when you have someone to give it to."

He smiled. "Does this mean you love me too?"

"I don't just love you, Joseph Rossi. I need you." She peppered his face with kisses. "I adore you." Her hands shook as she began unbuckling his belt. "I . . ."

"Allow me," he whispered, lifted her back off her feet, and carried her into his room, taking quiet care to lock the door behind him.

"You have an advantage over me," Molly said, as he deposited her in the middle of his bed.

His eyebrows arched, asking the question his lips did not.

"You've seen me naked," she said, her eyes twinkling. "It's about time you returned the favor."

Joseph grinned. "It will be my pleasure to accommodate you, my love," he said.

He did, and it was.

The bell over the shop door jingled. Harry paused in the middle of sweeping the floor and then grinned as the duo came into the shop, hand in hand.

"Hey there," Harry said. "It's good to see you guys." He set the broom aside and dusted his hands on the seat of his pants.

"I gots my siches out," Joey said, and brushed his hair away from his forehead.

"By golly, so you did!" Harry cried, and patted the child gently on top of the head. "I'll bet you didn't even cry."

Joseph hid a grin. "Not much," he offered, leaving out his son's hysterics.

Harry grinned. "Molly is in her office."

Joseph returned Harry's grin. "Am I that obvious?"

Harry shrugged. "Us men have to stick together, hunh, Joey?" And then he slapped his leg as if he'd just had a thought. "Say! I'll bet you'd like to go outside and see the new goldfish in the pond. One of them has a black tail."

Joey squealed and made a run for the back door. Harry looked up at Joseph for permission. "I'll keep an eye on him for you . . . if you need to see Molly."

I'll always need Molly, he thought. "Thanks," he said, "I appreciate the offer. Don't let him talk you into anything he's not supposed to do," he warned. Harry waved his concerns away and left with Joey firmly in hand.

Joseph walked down the hall toward Molly's office, pausing just inside the open doorway to feast his eyes on the sight of her. It had been exactly one day since they'd talked, and seven since they'd made love, and he was in desperate need of a fix. He needed Molly—to touch her, to hold her, to taste her laughter, to feel the love.

She was sitting at her desk, worrying her lower lip with the edge of her teeth, muttering under her breath as she stared at the monitor of her computer.

"Now, where did I put you?" she asked the screen, searching, as she had for the last forty-five minutes, for the lost invoice.

"You put me in need, lady," he said softly.

The hair stood up on the back of her neck as her hands went limp on the keys. Slowly, she swiveled herself around in the chair, praying she hadn't been imagining the voice that she'd heard.

A smile broke the solemnity of her face. "I didn't know you were coming." And then it froze in place as a thought occurred. "Is something wrong with Joey?"

"For a change, no," he said. "But there's something wrong with me."

He walked around her desk, pulled her to her feet and into his arms, nuzzling the spot beneath the lobe of her left ear that elicited the groan for which he'd been searching.

"What's wrong with you?" Molly asked. And then blushed when Joseph took her hand and slid it down the front of his slacks.

"Need I say more?" he asked.

"That's just an excuse you created on demand," she whispered, and slid her arms beneath his jacket.

The scent of leather, the familiar band of muscles across his back, and the laughter in his voice made her weak-kneed.

"That's not what we used to call it in high school," Joseph said, managing to keep a straight face in spite of the ache she'd started in his belly. Just looking at her made him want. And holding her created an impossible need for more.

"Oh, Lord, you're incorrigible," Molly said, and wrapped her arms around his neck.

"Nuh-uh," Joseph argued. "I'm as good and easy as it gets. All you have to do is say the word and I'm yours."

"The word," Molly said.

Joseph tilted his head back and laughed loud and long. "You just wait," he said. "You just wait until I can get you alone. I'll make you pay for this."

"Now Joseph, I know you're good . . . but I don't think you're good enough to start charging for—"

He stifled her remark with a kiss that started a fire of its own. And then nothing could be heard but a muffled moan and a shifting of feet across the office floor.

When he could think, he remembered why he'd come by. "Joey wanted to show you his head. He got his 'siches' out."

145

"Oh, dear, was it bad?" Molly asked, remembering what hell it had been just to put them in.

Joseph grinned. "Well, you know how interesting they've been to him, and how often he's looked at himself in a mirror to check their progress. All I can say is, giving them up wasn't easy."

"Then we'd better go see the little man," Molly said, as she led Joseph out of her office. "I need to be properly impressed. I'll bet he was an angel for the doctor."

Joseph grimaced. "You need to think again," he said. "He was hell on wheels."

"Just like his daddy," Molly said, and traced the length of the zipper on his pants lightly with the tip of her fingernail, and left Joseph standing in the middle of the hall with a silly smile on his face.

Molly came out the back door of her shop just as Joey tossed a handful of fish food into the water all at once.

"Hey, buddy," Molly called.

Joey pivoted and grinned. "Momma!" he cried, and ran toward the door, the fish forgotten in his need to show off his wound.

Molly scooped him up into her arms and planted a swift kiss on his cheek before he could object. "I heard you got your stitches out. Can I see?"

Joey nodded importantly. He swiped his hand

across his forehead, lifting his hair away from the tiny red mark, and frowned, trying to work up new indignation from the procedure.

"I'll bet you didn't even cry, did you?" Molly asked.

Truth warred with Joey's need to impress his favorite female. It came out somewhere in between when he answered.

"I cried . . . but not so loud," he said.

Molly nodded, trying desperately to keep a straight face.

"That's good. Big boys don't cry real loud." When she saw the concern on his face, she couldn't keep from whispering, "but they do cry, Joey. It's always okay to cry if you have to."

He nodded and started to stick his thumb in his mouth.

"Better wash your hands first," Molly said, as she grabbed the dirty little fist before the thought became deed. "You don't want to eat the fishes' food, do you?" The dry, dusty meal was all over his hands and shirt.

Harry grinned. "Come on, partner. Let's go wash, and then I'll bet I've got an extra quarter in my pocket. We'll put it in the gum machine and get us some gum, what do you say?"

"Yea!" Joey said, and made another run for the shop.

Harry had to hustle to keep up, and once again, Molly and Joseph were left alone.

"What will it take to get you to come over tonight and have dinner with us?" Joseph asked.

"An invitation."

"Consider yourself invited," he said, and then watched the way the blue in her eyes turned dark. She was all long legs and slender body, and he very badly wanted to strip her down and have his way with her.

She grinned and started toward him, her hair bouncing lightly upon her shoulders. The motion caught the hot rays of the afternoon sun, highlighting the auburn curls and framing her face in a halo of fire. Joseph's eyes narrowed as he watched her walk, remembering the fluidity of her body beneath him as they made love.

Molly slid her arms around his waist, hugging him just tight enough to reactivate the ache behind his zipper, and then slid her lips up the column of his throat, pausing at his chin long enough to make him worry that she was stopping there. She didn't. Her lips slid across his mouth and delicately nailed whatever he'd been about to say.

"Consider yourself warned," she whispered, and then followed Harry and Joey into the Garden of Eden.

For a long moment, Joseph was unable to move, and when he did, he looked around blindly, unaware whether or not he'd just made a fool of himself in front of God and everybody, then didn't care if he had. He turned around and stared at the sign across the back door of her shop and grinned at the implied meaning.

"The Garden of Eden . . . and Adam thought he had problems. I think I've just been handed a whole damn basket of temptation. And I can tell you now, I don't have the presence of mind to turn down one . . . single . . . solitary bite."

He stuffed his hands in his pockets, hoping that it would help hide the condition in which she'd left him, and walked toward the back door. He had to collect his child and his sanity before he could drive them both home.

Dear Miss Jordan,

I'm writing to you as one woman to another, simply to let you know that your son may not be cared for in the manner in which you believed when you relinquished custody. Please understand that I'm not passing judgment on what must have been a difficult decision for you to make, but I feel that you should know that another woman has come into your son's life who

149

may not be the best influence for him . . . or for Joey's father.

If you have any . . .

Marjorie finished rereading the letter she'd just composed, slid it into the preaddressed envelope, licked and then sealed it, tamping it lightly to insure that the glue had stuck. Making certain that the stamp was in place, she walked out of her house and toward the mailbox on the curb.

She didn't see the beauty of the fall flowers along her walk or smell the crisp tang of the first signs of autumn in the air. She didn't see her old neighbor across the street waving at her to come over for a visit. She was on a mission. She walked to the edge of the street, slipped the letter into her mailbox, and raised the red flag for the postman's notice.

"There, that does it," she said, and dusted her hands as if she'd just completed a dirty job.

In one respect she had, but the dirt was all on her. The letter she'd just written and mailed to one Carly Jordan was the first step she'd taken down the path of meddle. She'd never been on that particular path before, but Marjorie was certain that if she had, her husband would still be her husband and not her ex.

She smoothed a hand over the gray helmet of

her hair, found a place that needed some extra spray, and headed for her house with determination. Marjorie was big on propriety as well as people staying in their places. Everyone and everything had a place, and her hairdo was no exception.

"It's bedtime, buddy," Joseph said, as Joey made a mad dash through the living room, rolled across the throw pillows on the floor, and jumped to his feet and yelled, "Taa-daa!"

Molly rolled her eyes and tried not to laugh at the look of utter disgust on Joseph's face.

"No more taa-daas," Joseph said. "Pick up your toys and I'll be in to help you bathe and put on your pajamas."

Joey stuck out his lower lip and glared at his father's hard stare.

"Want Momma to do it," he said.

"Now, Joey. You know what—"

"It's all right," Molly said. "If it'll make things easier on both of you, I'm willing." She looked to Joseph for permission.

He shrugged and nodded. "I owe you," he said.

Molly smiled, slowly. "I'll collect later." Then before Joseph could respond, she turned toward his son and clapped her hands. "Race you," she shouted, and darted down the hall with Joey right behind her, squealing and shouting with every step.

Joseph didn't know whether to be glad that Joey loved Molly and had accepted her without batting an eye or worry that Molly was so taken with his son.

He told himself that he was being foolish, but he couldn't forget what she'd told him about not being able to have any more children.

What if she only loves me for my son? he asked himself. *Yeah, and what if you're just making excuses for yourself?* he thought. *You know that Molly cares for you, too. You're just jealous because she's going to give Joey a bath instead of giving one to you.*

He shoved his hands through his hair, then pivoted, unable to stay alone in the room with the feelings he couldn't control. He walked out of the house and onto the flagstone terrace, staring into the darkness and seeing nothing but an occasional night moth dive-bombing the yard light, remembering when he'd wished for someone to love and gotten nothing but another set of foster parents, then trying to forget that they'd been more of the same. As far as Joseph had been able to tell, most of his foster parents had considered him another paycheck rather than another child to help reach maturity with some illusions intact. Shadows darkened the yard—

and his eyes—as he tried not to remember anything else at all.

A siren sounded somewhere off in the distance.
A dog barked in a backyard three houses over.
And the sun set on another day in Oklahoma.

Molly leaned over, kissing Joey's soft cheek
and smiling to herself at the way he snuggled his
stuffed rabbit beneath his tummy. When he was
asleep, she slipped quietly out of his room.

Joseph was nowhere to be found. It took a few
minutes for her to think to look outside, and
when she did, she stood unobserved, watching
the play of emotions sweeping across his face as
the sun disappeared from view.

Her heart ached for his uncertainty, and for an
instant, she saw the child in the man. It was
enough to end her observation and send her outside and into his arms.

Molly slid her arms around him from behind,
laying her cheek against the place between his
shoulder blades and listening for the heartbeat
she knew was there.

"Are you all right?"

He smiled. "I am now. I didn't mean to leave
you alone for so long. I guess I got lost in thought.
Is Joey already in bed?"

"He's been asleep for nearly fifteen minutes,"
Molly said, and then she grinned. "But the bath-

room's a mess. He got more water on the floor than I got on him. However . . . he's clean and quiet. A woman couldn't ask for more."

"I could," Joseph said softly, and turned in her arms. "And I'm going to." His voice deepened, his grip tightened, and the air between them seemed charged. "Molly . . . why do you love me?"

She inhaled sharply. How could he not know?

Joseph continued, as if he'd never asked the first question. "I'm a man with a lot of baggage. Old problems, a new child, and a budding business that has yet to become a success. Not exactly the greatest catch on the block."

"My God," she said. "Is that how you see yourself?" Her fingers wrapped in the sleeves on his shirt and she resisted the urge to shake him. "I love you for a thousand reasons. I've never even stopped to disassemble them. They're all a part of you"—she paused, cupping his face in her hands—"just as I hope to be. I want to be a part of your life, whatever that means. I wish I had the right to wake up beside you each morning, and crawl into bed beside you each night. I wish I could point to you on a street and say, 'he's mine,' and know that it was the truth."

She stopped and shook her head. "You ask, why do I love you . . . better yet . . . why do you love me? I'm a broken woman, Joseph. I can love, I can even make love. But I'll never be able to make babies with you. I'll never be able to feel the love we share grow inside of me. What do you think about that?"

He was stunned by her lecture, and the truth of her words. But he knew in the instant that it was voiced that nothing would matter if they could be together.

"I think that you've been cheated out of something you desperately want. But you've got to believe that the only thing I want or need from you is love . . . the knowledge that you'll always be there for me . . . and"—he smiled, and caressed her cheek with the tip of a finger—"our son. Remember, you're already someone's 'momma.' "

Her sob came quickly, unexpectedly. Molly shuddered, then buried her face in her hands, too moved to allow him to see her vulnerability.

"Ah, God," Joseph whispered. "I didn't mean to make you cry."

"It wasn't from sadness," she whispered. "It was just that dose of overwhelming love that took me by surprise."

Joseph scooped her up into his arms. "If you think that felt good, wait till you see what's next."

Molly buried her head against his shoulder. "Don't forget to lock the door," she said, as he carried her back inside the house. "I won't be going out again tonight."

That could only mean one thing. She'd finally succumbed to his pleas to stay the night. "Molly . . . are you sure? I don't want you to feel pressured by what I said."

"Are you going to respect me in the morning?" she asked shyly.

"Not unless I actually have to," he teased. "I'd a whole lot rather. . . . " He leaned down and whispered in her ear.

It was dark and quiet inside his house, yet he heard her gasp and saw her blush. But he should have known he'd never get the better of her.

"Is that a one-time offer?" she asked. "Or can I have seconds?"

"Oh, woman!" He laughed softly as he lifted her up into his arms. "I promise I'll die trying," he said, and carried her into his room.

↫ Seven

"You can't fire me. I quit!"

Carly Jordan slammed the files she was holding onto the desk and glared at the man behind it, daring him to make a scene.

Marcus Huddson shrugged. Whatever it took, seeing the last of her would be good riddance.

"And furthermore," Carly said, "ruining my reputation to get back at me won't wash. You shouldn't have played dirty with me, Marcus, then I wouldn't have been forced to do this."

She yanked an envelope of photos from her purse, tossed them on top of the files scattered across his desk, and smirked with satisfaction as the blood slowly drained from her boss's face.

"What are you doing with these?" he gasped, unwilling to even touch the pictorial reminders of their illicit affair. "When did you have these taken?"

He looked down at them in horror and then back up at the woman before him, wondering what he'd ever seen in her. Suddenly her tall, Scandinavian beauty had turned into something hideous and evil.

"*I'm* not doing anything with them," Carly said. "I have no idea what your wife's plans are, but I'm sure they don't include me. After all, I have nothing left to lose. You've already made that perfectly clear."

"Oh God," Marcus Huddson groaned. Then temper overcame panic. "You bitch!" he whispered. "I'll make you sorry."

Carly shrugged. "I'm already sorry. I should have stayed with Peter, not you. He's much better in bed, and even though he's not vice president, he's still the CEO's nephew."

Marcus Huddson blanched. He'd met some conniving women in his day, but none who were so blatantly willing to admit that sleeping their way to the top beat all-out work every time.

"You'll never work in the computer industry again," Huddson warned. "I'll see to that."

Carly leaned forward, giving her ex-lover a bird's-eye view of her ample cleavage, and whispered, "I don't intend to try, Marcus darling.

And"—she smiled viciously—"I'll bet I have another job before you can find another wife."

She left on her exit line, slamming the door behind her, then quickly emptied her desk and walked out of the corporate offices of TXX Computers with her head held high.

She fumed all the way to her town house apartment and, when she'd entered her home, she tossed the personal belongings she'd emptied from her desk and let her emotions fly.

"Damn! Damn! Damn!"

Tears poured as temper raged. A vase she'd purchased in Rangoon last year shattered against the dining room wall. Good china she'd picked up on her last trip to England went in all directions. There was no stopping the rage once she let it overwhelm her. Most times Carly Jordan refused to admit it, but the fact was, the one and only thing she could not control was herself.

When there was nothing left within reaching distance to break, she flung herself down upon the sofa and stared blankly at the muted ceiling lights, trying to think of a plan. Minutes passed as the adrenaline rush subsided, and when she could think without seething, one clear, conscious thought emerged.

"Enrique Salazar!"

The dark-eyed Latin who'd tried unsuccessfully to woo her away from Marcus during their last cruise had lingered in her mind as well as something he'd whispered in her ear during a midnight dance. Something about persuasion and promises and all the lovemaking she could handle.

"What did I do with his card?" Carly muttered, heading for the drawer in the hall table where she usually put such things.

Mail lay at her feet, having been pushed through the drop slot in her door earlier in the day. She tossed it onto the table and then began to dig through the drawer. Fury renewed as she searched in vain.

"Damn!" She glared down at the stack of mail, knowing that it probably contained bills she would not be able to pay, then tried to think where the card could be.

Losing the connection to the man in black could be serious, and remembering his dark Spanish eyes and the way he'd been unable to keep his hands off of her delicate white skin and her ash blond hair renewed the vigor of her search.

For several hours, Carly's apartment and everything in it suffered total destruction before she remembered the jewelry pouch. Retracing her search of her bedroom, it didn't take long to find it, and when she did, tore into it with delight.

"Yes, Carly, you are a jewel!" she shrieked, laughing at her own pun. When she'd worn out the humor of the situation, she paced the floor in her bedroom, tapping the edge of the card against her lower lip as she began to formulate a new plan. "Now, Enrique, my darling, how do I go about letting you know that I couldn't get you out of my mind?"

With focused, single-minded intent, Carly Jordan sat with pen in hand and began to compose one of her more striking efforts at persuasion. An hour and two drafts later, she sat back with a firm smile on her face.

"Enrique Salazar, if you can resist this heartrending plea, then you're not the man I need."

She slipped the letter into a pale mauve envelope, sprayed a whiff of perfume into the air and then quickly waved the envelope in and out of the fragrant mist before affixing a stamp in the corner. Two steps down the hall from her front door was a postal drop. She hesitated at the slot, making the mailing something of an event.

"Here's to carnal knowledge, my darling," she sneered. "Forever may it reign."

The envelope disappeared down the chute and Carly did likewise into her room. It was three days later before she remembered the mail she'd tossed aside, and then another four before she spared the time to look. By this time, a staggering accumulation of letters were staring her in the face, as was the fact that next month's rent was due and she was nearly broke. All she could do was pray that Enrique Salazar was as good as his promises.

She sat down at her desk, checking to make certain that everything she needed was there before her. The letter opener was at hand, as was the wastebasket, and a vodka gimlet. If one didn't work, the latter certainly couldn't hurt.

One by one, Carly slit, read, and dispensed. There was little she could do with the major bills. She'd lived beyond her means for years and depended on the generosity of her "friends" for the rest. The bills she threw away. The wastebasket filled as she emptied the drink. And then she came to a single plain envelope with no return address, no company name, nothing but an Oklahoma City postmark. She frowned, opened it, and began to read.

"What in the . . . ?"

That she was startled was putting it mildly. It had been over three years since she'd seen this name in print, and almost as long since she'd even given it—or him—a thought.

"Well, well, well! So, Joseph my love, what

have you gone and done? Attached yourself to someone unsuitable? That doesn't sound like you."

She frowned, remembering the one time in her life she'd experienced true fear. Joseph Rossi had been the only man in her life she'd loved more than herself, and the only one she couldn't control.

"We would have been perfect together," she muttered. "You were good in bed, destined to be successful, and gorgeous to boot. You just couldn't get past your own damned childhood . . . or lack thereof . . . could you, Joseph, darling? If you'd let me take care of our little . . . 'problem' . . . my way . . . I wouldn't be having any of *these* problems now."

She shuddered, remembering Joseph's fury at her attempt to schedule an abortion. She'd been scared enough to chance ruining her figure and give birth, just for the opportunity to keep breathing. The whole process of childbirth had been disgusting. What she'd felt for Joseph Rossi had died when the child was born. She'd done all she could to thrust it, and him, from her mind forever—until now.

The letter was vague, mostly ramblings about the despair that Carly must be suffering at losing her child and how distraught she must be that said child was growing up without a proper mother's love.

She rolled her eyes at the thought of kids in general and wondered again who could have known about her connection to Joseph—or sent the letter.

"Ugh," she muttered. "Nothing but dirty pants and dirty faces and unending noise." She frowned, crumpled the letter into a wad, and tossed it into the wastebasket along with the rest of her life that she couldn't deal with.

The phone rang, and for a long, long moment, she considered letting her machine pick up the message. But she'd learned long ago that men hated to leave personal messages on such things, and she was in dire need of anything male and personal.

"Hello?" Her voice was low, sultry, and perfectly practiced. And then the sex slid out of her voice and a screech moved into place. "Well, the same to you, buddy," she screamed. "If I don't have the money, I can't pay. It's as simple as that. When I get it, you get it, until then, no deal. *Get it?*"

She slammed down the phone, buried her face in her hands, and moaned. Long strands of silky blond hair fell across her fingers as she thrust them angrily against her scalp. They caught and then pulled as they tangled in one of the rings she was wearing.

"Ouch!" she cried, then jerked, which only served to catch her hair tighter. She slid the ring from her finger. "Damn it. I should have tossed this years ago."

She muttered and cursed again, and then finally managed to work the hair out of the ring's setting. As she turned it toward the light, she stared, remembering the man and the occasion. Remembering that when she and Joseph had split, she'd kept the ring strictly for selfish, rather than sentimental, reasons.

"But . . . he doesn't know that," she told herself. The simple opal and topaz ring reflected the late afternoon light, winking and sparkling as she turned it first one way and then another. "As far as Joseph Rossi will know, I kept this out of undying love." She stared at the wastebasket overflowing with unpaid bills and then back at the ring. She thought of the answer she was expecting from Enrique Salazar and shrugged.

"I'll leave a forwarding address . . . just in case I get lucky. Joseph, darling, I've just decided that I can't live another day without you and our son." She smiled, but the joy did not reach her eyes. "And you *are* so very, very good in bed."

* * *

Molly slammed her car into PARK, grabbed the keys and the box on the seat beside her, and made a run for Joseph's office. She winced as her ankle caught the edge of the elevator door and tried not to curse as a pain shot all the way to her knee.

"Shoot," she muttered, and leaned down to rub it. "Joey Rossi, If I didn't love you and your daddy so much, I wouldn't be doing this."

The elevator stopped, and Molly bolted out through the doors as soon as they opened, continuing her mad dash toward Joseph's office.

Marjorie Weeks looked up and frowned as the door banged sharply against the inner wall, glaring at the woman who came in on the run.

"Miss Eden." Censure was thick in her voice.

Molly sighed. No matter how hard she tried, she'd yet to make a good impression on this woman.

"Sorry," she said, and shut the door more carefully than when she'd come in. "I'm late, and I didn't want to keep Joseph waiting."

"Mr. Rossi is on the phone," Marjorie said. "If you'll just have a seat, he'll be out shortly."

Molly nodded, then sat down, balancing the box carefully on her jeans-clad knees as she unzipped the top of her jacket. She caught Joseph's secretary staring at the box on her lap, and she smiled, hoping that this might be a key to break-ing the ice between them.

"Cookies," she said.

"Excuse me?" Marjorie Weeks said.

Molly pointed to the box. "I said, I brought Joey's cookies." Then Molly continued as if the woman had expressed an interest in hearing more, when in actuality, she'd done exactly the opposite. "Today is the Halloween party at Joey's day care and Joseph forgot he'd promised to bring cookies. He called me about an hour ago. I called four bakeries before I found one that still had Halloween cookies for sale."

"If I'd known he needed cookies, I could have baked them myself," Marjorie said shortly. "I'm quite good at it, you know. I took a special course."

Molly's eyebrows rose, but she wisely did nothing other than nod knowledgeably. "They had to be in the shape of pumpkins," Molly of-fered.

"I have jack-o'-lantern cookie cutters in two sizes," Mrs. Weeks said.

"I wish we'd known," Molly said softly. "Yours would have been much more special to Joey than these . . . but we didn't think. Sorry . . . maybe next time . . . say Christmas?"

Marjorie's eyes lit up. For the first time since

she and Molly met, a kind thought about her surfaced. A person couldn't be all bad who went to so much trouble for a child. She absorbed Molly's offer and finally answered, pursing her lips as she nodded.

"Maybe Christmas," she agreed.

"Molly, thank God you're here!"

Joseph's exit from his office was less than orderly. He leaned down, swooped the box of cookies from her lap, and started toward the door when he turned, came back and kissed her on the cheek. "And you're a lifesaver! Thank you, thank you, thank you."

She tried not to gape at his dimples and gave it up as a lost cause. When he smiled, he was impossible to ignore. "Don't thank me. The bakery at Homeland was your lifesaver. I was just the delivery boy."

Joseph couldn't help admiring her long-limbed grace as she uncoiled herself from the chair, and then grinned as she tried unsuccessfully to smooth down her unruly curls.

"And one of the prettiest delivery boys I ever saw. Don't you agree, Mrs. Weeks?"

Marjorie sniffed and managed a smile that seemed to satisfy her boss.

"I'll be back within the hour," he told his secretary. "Right now, I've got to buy my way out of a broken promise. Two dozen pumpkins coming up." He blew Molly a kiss and then he was gone, leaving a faint scent of sugar cookies and Stetson cologne behind him.

Molly and Mrs. Weeks stared at each other, then each looked away. There had to be some common ground somewhere between these two women, but for the life of her, Molly couldn't find it, and Marjorie Weeks didn't seem willing to look.

"I suppose I'd better be going," Molly said. "I still have a lot of deliveries to make, and I don't want to leave Cora alone at the shop too long. She's having arthritis really bad these days. I think it's the change in weather."

Marjorie's perfectly arched and drawn eyebrows peaked. She was surprised that this woman seemed sincerely concerned about one of her employee's comforts. Since Marjorie had suffered some similar complaints, she knew how miserable the pain could be. She watched Molly leave without further comment, but wondered, as the door went shut, if possibly—just possibly— she had misjudged her.

The memory of that letter she'd sent weeks ago to Carly Jordan surfaced, along with a definite twinge that she recognized as guilty conscience. Quickly, she turned to her desk, busying herself with the letters she had to transcribe, and pushed all worries out of her mind. After all, there was surely no need to fuss about that silly little letter. It had been so long. If the child's mother was going to come, she'd have already been here and gone.

"Daddy!" Joey shrieked, as Joseph walked into the center with the bakery box in his hands.

Joseph grinned, handed the box to Lila Forshee, and bent down and scooped Joey into his arms.

"My punkins!" Joey yelled at his friends, and pointed importantly to Lila's box. "Daddy broughts my punkins!"

Joseph grinned, stole a quick kiss, and then plopped his son down on the floor. "Thanks to Molly," he told Lila.

Lila grinned. "You seem to be doing that a lot these days," she teased.

"What's that?" he asked.

"Thanking Molly."

Joseph smiled softly. "Among other things," he said. And then he grew serious. "Frankly, I don't know what Joey and I would have done without her. She's become a very, very important person in our lives."

"I'm glad to hear that," Lila said. "Molly's a

nice person. I'd hate to see her hurt—again." She saw Joseph's surprised expression. "We've known each other since college. I know the whole story. It wasn't her fault. He had all of us fooled."

Joseph frowned, his voice was just above a growl. "Don't look at me. I'd kill before I willingly hurt that woman. And I wish—just once— for the chance to meet up with the SOB who *did* hurt her."

Lila touched his arm. "Probably just as well if you don't."

The children's shrieks of excitement grew as one of the workers entered the dining area clothed in a sheet.

"I'd better go, now," she said. "The ghost is here. If I don't miss my guess, between too much excitement and too much sugar, I won't get a single child down for a nap."

Joseph laughed. "Thanks for the warning. I'll know what to expect when I pick him up this evening."

Lila waved good-bye as he made a hasty exit. Joey didn't even know that he was gone.

Joseph stood outside the door for a moment, looking back inside at the happy chaos of the children who ran wildly around the ghost who'd taken a seat in the center of the room. Joey was right in the thick of things, laughing and pushing his way into place. And he wasn't even sucking his thumb. Joseph sighed. His son was growing up. And the holidays that signaled the end of a year kept coming closer and closer. One of these days, he was going to pin Molly Eden down to a happy-ever-after.

The wind whipped around the corner of her house just as Molly opened the front door. Her blue jeans and new white sweater were warm, and would be fine once she was at work. But the jacket she had on was no match for this biting wind. She shivered and made a U-turn in the doorway, trading the jacket for a heavy parka hanging in the hall closet instead. It was only the first week of November, but already Oklahoma City was experiencing its first taste of winter weather.

She looked up at the cold, gray skies, thinking that the predicted snow flurries might just pass them by if the front didn't come too far south, and headed for her car. There was no need to second-guess the weather. It did what it was going to do, and she did what she had to, to cope.

As she backed out of her driveway, she glanced at Joseph's house out of habit. It was old but stately, and it would look wonderful with a huge wreath of evergreens hanging on the front door—

and maybe a big, fluffy red bow and some pine cones hot-glued in place. She could just picture it now. Refusing to admit that she was fantasizing about something that wasn't hers, she headed for the Garden of Eden. It was time to go to work.

Carly Jordan pulled over to the curb, glancing down at the map of Oklahoma City on the seat beside her, then back up at the numbers of the house across the street.

"So . . . here's where you disappeared to," she muttered, as she circled the location of Joseph's house on her map. "You're an awfully long way from Natchez, darling. What on earth were you running from? Me, I hope."

A woman exited the house where Carly had parked. When she saw her come out, she started to pull away, and then an intense curiosity, as well as the urge to know all the answers before the questions were asked, prompted Carly to get out and strike up a conversation.

"Hello," Carly said brightly. "I wonder if you might be able to help me? I'm looking for Joseph Rossi's house. By any chance do you know where he lives? I think I'm in the right neighborhood, but I'm just not certain about—"

"Why, you're here and don't know it," the woman cried. She pointed across the street.

"That's it. The one with the hedge. Are you family? He has the sweetest little boy. And the way he looks after him is so wonderful. It's not often you find a father who's also a single parent, you know." She winked to make her point.

Carly smiled thinly. Even hearing about the child's existence still angered her, as did the fact that Joseph was actually managing quite well alone.

"Of course," the woman continued, as if Carly had participated in the conversation, "it probably won't be long before his 'single' status changes."

Carly's attention fine-tuned through the gossip to the stuff she might use. "Are you saying that he's dating?" she asked.

"I guess that's what they call it these days," the woman said. "And it's just too convenient for words."

"What do you mean, convenient?" Carly asked.

"He's been keeping company with the girl next door," the woman said. "She's a real sweet thing. I've known her all her life. Why, her mother and I were the best of—"

"What's her name?" Carly asked, staring at the house next door, trying to imagine Joseph and anyone in the throes of passion, and decided the image pissed her off.

"Molly Eden," the woman said. "She owns a flower shop called the Garden of Eden—get it? Eden . . . Garden of . . ."

In the middle of the dialogue, Carly turned and walked back to the car, slid behind the wheel, and drove away. She didn't bother to look back. If she had, she would have seen an expression of surprise on the woman's face. But she wouldn't have cared. What she'd learned wasn't the best of news. But at least there would be fewer surprises when she got down to business.

"So . . . there's a Miss Molly in your life, my dear, dear Joseph." Carly's face was angry as she turned the corner. "Exactly where will she figure in my plans . . . and better yet . . . how can I use her to my advantage?"

Carly headed down the street, searching for a clean but less-than-ostentatious motel, and decided that another day of reconnoitering before the surprise attack wouldn't hurt.

"Marjorie, I'll be out nearly all day on consultations." Joseph handed his secretary a sheaf of papers to file. "When you've finished with these, take an early lunch and treat yourself to a little time off. You've earned it."

"But what about the office?"

"Turn on the answering machine, stick a sign

on the door telling whoever comes knocking what time you'll be back, and go buy something frivolous."

She smiled. It was a rare, ingenuous smile, and for just a moment, Joseph imagined what she'd looked like as a young woman, before life and its disappointments had marked her face.

"Maybe I will," she said. "I could do a little early Christmas shopping. I hate to wait until later when the stores are so crowded. It gives me claustrophobia."

Joseph waved good-bye, leaving Marjorie with a sense of anticipation she hadn't had in months.

Less than thirty minutes later, she looked up from her filing, smiled absently at the woman who entered the office, and then nearly died on the spot.

"Carly Jordan to see Joseph Rossi, please," the woman said.

Oh no! Marjorie thought. *Not now!*

Marjorie absorbed the full effect of the expensive suit, the stylish hair, and the beautiful face of the woman in front of her before she was able to speak. She seemed cool and distant, but Marjorie was willing to give the woman the benefit of the doubt. After all, Joseph had seen fit to love her. She'd borne them a child. There had to be passion behind that cool facade.

"I'm so sorry, but he's going to be out most of the day. I'm not even certain that he'll come back to the office before closing. He may go straight to day care to pick up his child and then home."

The moment it was out of her mouth, she gasped, realizing what she'd said, and waited for the woman's show of emotion—but it never came. No tears, not even a glimmer of remorse. Only a narrowing of those silvery green eyes.

Damn, Carly thought. *This changes everything.* She slipped a perfect smile in place and shrugged for added effect. "Maybe I'll try to meet up with him at the day-care center. Could you give me the address?"

The question was unnecessary, but the secretary didn't need to know that. Carly'd been in town for two days and had scoped the entire situation thoroughly, down to the fact that Joseph's next-door neighbor meant more to him than was absolutely necessary. She'd already planned a use for such knowledge. Carly Jordan smiled to herself. She always had a contingency plan.

Marjorie was in a quandary. Knowing who the woman was put a completely different light on what she was about to do. But, she told herself, there's no way anyone could know that she was the one who sent the letter. And what harm could there be in inadvertently telling a woman where

177

her own child was? It wasn't as if she'd asked about the child, anyway. She'd simply asked for a place to catch up with Joseph.

Marjorie sighed, wrote down the address of the center, and handed it over, hoping to see past the coolness to the mother beneath. She couldn't see a thing except a tiny smear on Carly Jordan's jacket.

"Thank you," Carly said shortly, and stuffed the address in her handbag. She started out the door and then turned and flashed her famous, million-dollar smile. "I'm sure we'll be seeing each other again. You don't know what this means to me."

Marjorie gawked. There was nothing else she could do. And for some reason, the pleasure of her intended shopping expedition had suddenly disappeared. She slumped down in the chair behind her desk and stared at the telephone, willing it not to ring. She was in no mood to conduct business today.

Joseph sighed as he turned into the parking lot of the day-care center and then smiled, remembering that later, he and Joey would be guests at Molly's for some of her famous lasagna. It was their favorite food.

He got out of his car, then caught his breath at

the chill of the wind that swooped down the collar of his jacket.

"Damn," he muttered. "Natchez was never like this." However, returning to Mississippi, the state in which he'd been raised, was no longer a possibility. When he'd left, he'd willingly cut all ties, for his sake as well as Joey's. He headed for the front door at a jog.

"Why, Mr. Rossi! I didn't expect to see you again today."

The girl at the front desk giggled, and then looked away, trying not to appear as eager as she actually was to see this particular father. In her opinion he was too gorgeous for words. And although she'd only worked here two weeks, she prided herself that she already knew every parent by sight and name.

"Why ever not?" he asked. "Unless you're having a sale on kids and mine was the first to go?" The laughter in his voice died with the smile on her face.

She stuttered, "W-why . . . because . . . because Joey's not here," she said. "I signed him out myself . . . over two hours ago."

Joseph's heart jerked. He couldn't think fast enough to ask. He needn't have bothered. The girl was offering way more information than necessary to make right what she'd done.

179

"It was done properly," she said, and for a moment, looked nervously away. "I know the rules when someone other than a parent comes to pick them up. I always check their files."

"Who took him?" Joseph asked.

The girl stuttered, grabbed for the guest register, and pointed, "W-why . . . your friend, Molly Eden. I've never met her personally, but I've heard all about her . . . especially from Joey. How he calls her his mother . . . and how you've given her permission to pick him up when you're late. I just assumed that you knew."

Joseph sighed, partly from relief, partly from exasperation. He couldn't imagine why Molly would do something so outrageous, but at least his son was safe.

"May I use your phone?" he asked, and picked it up without waiting for an answer.

He dialed, frowned when there was no answer at her home, and tried the florist shop instead. Why Molly would take Joey there if she wasn't finished work was beyond him. The boy could take Wal-Mart apart if given enough time. He'd make hash of that shop full of breakables.

Molly answered on the third ring. Joseph could tell by the breathless quality of her voice that she'd run to answer it. He could just imagine why.

"Molly . . . it's me," he said shortly.

"Well, hi!" she said. The unexpected pleasure of hearing his voice made her pulse accelerate. "What's up? Please don't tell me you're going to be late, because I'm starved. I skipped lunch in honor of you guys and my lasagna." She smiled to herself, expecting to hear a familiar chuckle. The anger in his voice surprised her.

"I won't be late . . . in fact, I came to day care early to pick Joey up. I wish you'd told me you were going to get him. It would have saved me an unnecessary drive."

Molly's stomach turned. "I don't know what you mean," she whispered.

Joseph was so caught up in his anger that at first he didn't catch the implication of her words. "I mean . . . that the next time you intend to pick Joey up . . . clear it with me first, okay?"

"Oh God," Molly whispered, and dropped backward into a chair. "Joseph, listen to me! I swear . . . I don't have Joey. I haven't seen him since yesterday."

Joseph paled, his hands began to shake, and his voice deepened. "What do you mean . . . you don't have him? The new girl . . ." He turned to the receptionist and all but yelled at her, "What's your name?"

"Sheila," she whimpered. She'd already decided that something was very definitely wrong.

"Sheila says you signed Joey out. Please Molly, this isn't funny."

Molly's chin trembled. She couldn't bear to think of the implications of this news. Children were snatched everyday. She'd just never expected to know one.

"I don't know a 'Sheila.' I haven't been to the center in weeks, Joseph. And you know I wouldn't tease . . . not about this. Look at the name again. Maybe it isn't mine. Maybe she's mixed me up with someone else and Joey's actually still there."

Joseph looked and then groaned. "It's your name . . . but . . . oh Jesus, Molly, it's not your writing."

Molly gasped.

"Look," Joseph said. "I've got to go. I'll call you later, or something. I've got to find Joey." He hung up.

Molly stared at the phone in her hand as if it had suddenly grown fangs.

Cora took one look at Molly's face, set the fresh floral arrangement she'd been working on into the cooler for customer viewing, and grabbed Molly by the shoulders.

"What's wrong?" she asked.

Pale and shaking, it took Molly several deep breaths before she could speak the ugliness of what she'd learned.

"That was Joseph. Someone checked Joey out of the day-care center and used my name. No one seems to know where he is."

"Oh my God!" Cora gasped.

"Look," Molly said, "I've got to go. I can't sit here and wait for Joseph to call. Besides, whether I like it or not, I've been implicated in this. If the police show up . . . and they probably will . . . I want to talk to them myself, not have them come looking for me. Understand?"

Cora threw her arms around Molly's neck and then pressed a swift kiss on her cheek.

"Let us know what's happening," she said. And then she turned away, unwilling for Molly to see the tears. She was already frightened enough as it was. "He's such a dear little boy, I can't bear to think of anything awful happening to him."

"Say a prayer," Molly said.

And then she was gone.

∽ *Eight*

Lila Forshee burst through the door of her office and out into the foyer of the center. She'd heard the shouting through two closed doors and above the humming of the central heat.

"What in the world is wrong out here?" she asked, taking in Sheila's hysteria and Joseph's dark, forbidding expression in one long look.

"Joey's missing," Joseph said shortly.

Lila's heart all but stopped. The horror of all people who care for children had just come home to roost.

"No!" she cried. "How could this happen, Sheila? Surely you didn't let him go with just anyone?"

Sheila was in tears. "No, of course not," she sobbed. "I checked the files. The woman said her name was Molly Eden. Molly Eden's name is on the list of people allowed to see the Rossi child."

Lila sighed. "There you have it," she said. "If Molly has him, then I'm sure he's fine."

Sheila began to blubber. "He already called," she cried. "She doesn't."

Lila tried not to let her panic show. "Let me think. What did the woman look like who took Joey? You know how he is. He wouldn't go with a stranger. How did he act?"

Sheila blew her nose forcefully and tried desperately to remember. "Well . . . Joey kept saying he wanted his mother. . . ." She shook her head. "No . . . that's not exactly right. He said he wanted 'momma.' "

Joseph sighed. None of this made sense. That's what Joey called Molly. Momma . . . not mother.

"Why was he asking for Molly if she was already there?" Lila muttered.

Joseph exploded. "That's just the goddamned point. Molly wasn't here." He pointed to Sheila. "She let a total stranger take away my son." He made pivoted in frustration and then buried his face in his hands. "Oh God, don't let this be happening."

Sheila promptly burst back into more tears. Lila felt herself getting sick. This was a nightmare.

"Okay, enough of that for the moment," she said sharply. "Joseph . . . is there anyone . . . maybe your mother or a sister . . . someone who came to town that you don't know about who'd take Joey, thinking to surprise you?"

"I don't have a mother or a sister," he said shortly. "If someone was planning a surprise, why did they use someone else's name to take my son? Why, Lila? Why?"

Lila frowned. "I'm calling the police. In the meantime, Sheila, get yourself together and start trying to remember what the woman looked like. Stop sniveling—and I mean now! You can cry later, after we've found Joey."

Sheila nodded, started to speak, and then pointed to the front door of the center and screamed.

"There! That's the woman! And—oh, thank you, Lord—she has Joey with her!" She slumped into her chair, buried her face in her hands, and cried some more, only this time from sheer relief.

Joseph spun, his gaze intently fixed upon the tall blond who'd just entered the center, and then stared down at the small, dark-haired child struggling to get out of her grip.

"Oh . . . my . . . God!" It was all he was able to say.

Carly Jordan was caught unawares. Her carefully laid plans had been going awry ever since she'd picked up this demon from hell. And she'd never intended to get caught like this. She'd planned to take the child, form an instant rapport so that she could insinuate herself back into Joseph's life, and then throw herself on the mercy of him and the court.

Well, shit! she thought. *If I'm going to do any mercy throwing, now's the time.* The look on his face was similar to the one he'd worn when he'd caught her making an appointment for the abortion that never was.

She lowered her voice to a dramatic gasp, dropped her tight-fisted hold on Joey's wrist, and threw herself into Joseph's arms.

"Joseph, darling! I thought I'd never find you!"

Joseph struggled with the woman and her grasping hands, while fury exploded inside his head. He'd known her too long to fall for this stunt. He'd also known her well enough and long enough to recognize her panic when she'd walked into the center and realized she'd been found out.

"Get off of me." His voice was just shy of vicious as he unwound her arms from around his neck and shoved her aside. "I need to see my son."

Carly sniffed delicately into a lace-edged handkerchief, and cast the shocked audience a despairing glance. "He's my son, too," she said, and then added several sobs for effect.

"No!"

Molly's agonized whisper split the tension. She closed her eyes and clutched the side of the door for support. *This can't be happening again*, she thought. *I can't have fallen for another man who lied to me like . . .*

When Joseph realized Molly had seen and heard everything, he felt sick. *Oh my God! With her history, she'll never trust me again.* But he desperately needed her to believe him. Without Molly, he and Joey had nothing.

"Don't, Molly! It's not what you think, and thank God you're here."

She shuddered, then swayed. Her eyes locked with Joseph's gaze of entreaty. She thought he'd been different.

"Molly, darling . . . don't!" He'd seen the look on her face and knew what she was thinking, but it was all he could think to say.

She took a deep breath. If he was willing to call her that, before witnesses, then the least she could do was calm down and give them all a chance. And then she remembered Joey. He must be terrified.

Simultaneously, she and Joseph looked down

at the small child who stood backed against the wall, a lot uncertain and a little frightened of the hubbub around him.

He sniffed, gave Molly and Joseph a brown, watery gaze, and stuffed his thumb in his mouth as his father knelt at his feet.

"Are you all right, fella?" Joseph's hands made frantic forays across the tiny child's body, as if to assure himself that he was truly there.

"Gots sick," Joey said, pointing to the messy condition of his clothes.

"Yes, you did, didn't you," Molly said. "Let's go get cleaned up while Daddy talks to his friends, okay?" She wouldn't—couldn't—look at Joseph. If he wore a guilty expression, she'd die right here in front of God and everybody and she wasn't ready to do that—not just yet.

Joey nodded, unstuck his thumb, and willingly clasped Molly's hand as she led him away.

Joseph frowned at the stiffness of Molly's retreating figure. But there was time later to sort all of this out. Right now, he had another problem on his hands, and he knew he wasn't dealing with it, or her, alone. He stood and turned, fixing Carly with a hard, pointed glare.

"Lila, call the police!"

Carly blanched. This wasn't going according to plan. First the child had all but gutted her with his heels. He'd stuffed his face with all the food she'd used as persuasion, and then he'd thrown up all over her and her rental car, refusing to even talk to her again. And then, to make matters worse, he'd run into that bitch's arms the moment she walked into the room.

"Joseph!" Carly gasped, hoping that she sounded properly shocked. "You can't mean it! You wouldn't have your own child's mother arrested?"

"You're not his mother," he said shortly. "You were just the delivery bag. I'm Joey's mother . . . and father. By your own choice, you are nothing. Not now, not ever. Now sit down and shut up, and let me think."

She collapsed into a chair, sobbing prettily, and hoped the police who arrived were young and good-looking. At least then she'd have something to work with.

Molly turned the water on full blast, letting it drown out the sounds of anger beyond the door as she cleaned Joey up as best she could.

His eyes were huge, and the tears were brimming. His lower lip quivered and he kept pulling his hand away from Molly's ministrations with the wet paper towels in an endeavor to stuff his much-needed thumb back into his mouth.

"Just a minute," she said softly, "and we'll be

through. Then you can chew on that thing all you want."

She winked to lighten her words and when she was finished, popped it into his mouth for him, smiling in response to his delighted giggle. She swooped him into her arms and hugged him tightly, ignoring the smell still on his clothes. They stank. There was only so much that liquid soap and water could do; after that, a change of clothes was in order.

"Let's go find Daddy," she told him. "You need to go home."

In her absence, the police had arrived upon the scene. She walked into the lobby and into the middle of angry voices. Instantly, Joey buried his face against her neck, hiding his face from the noise, and started whimpering. Like her, he'd had enough, and she knew it was only a matter of time before he started a major set of tears.

"I don't know what anyone else thinks," she said, "but Joey and I have had all of this we can stand, so if no one minds, I'll take him home and get him changed." She couldn't look at Joseph. It would hurt too much if she saw regret in his eyes. She wasn't ready to contemplate losing this man—or his child—not just yet.

"Not so fast," an officer said, restraining Molly with a look.

The police officer was already in over his head with explanations, and now another set of people he knew nothing about had appeared, announcing an exit. He wasn't about to let them go.

"It's okay, Officer," Joseph said. "That's the real Molly Eden. She's my neighbor, and she's always had my permission to take my son home."

"My momma," Joey said, hugged Molly, and sniffed again.

The officer looked startled.

"Don't ask," Joseph said with a weary grin.

The officer nodded and made a note of Molly's name and address for future reference, as well as her place of business.

Molly called Cora to tell her Joey had been found, then left with the child in her arms, unable to look back to see if anyone was watching. She didn't want to think about her future with Joseph. Today, it could very well have gone to hell.

"Come on, darling," she said softly, making sure that Joey was safely buckled up. "Let's get you home and changed. You stink."

He nodded. "I stink," he repeated.

She laughed—it was impossible not to—and then winced as his dimples came and went. Everything about him was so like his father—the skunk.

* * *

Joseph rubbed a shaky hand across his forehead, ignoring the threatening headache as he pulled out of the police parking lot and into traffic. Willingly, he'd gone down to headquarters, made a statement, and then waited what seemed to be forever before he could sign the complaint. All he wanted was to get to Molly and explain.

Too fed up to even think about what Carly had done, he was more than ready to leave her fate up to the authorities. Later, as he pulled into his driveway, his stomach turned, certain that he was in for yet another argument, and wearily pocketed his keys before entering the house.

Molly tiptoed out of Joey's room, shut the door all but a crack, and started toward the kitchen to fix herself something to drink. Joey was clean and changed, and he'd passed out for a nap without an argument. As long as Thumper was beneath his belly and his thumb was in his mouth, all was right with Joey's world.

Her steps dragged with exhaustion as she came through the kitchen door. The last thing she expected to see was Joseph leaning against the kitchen cabinet, nor did she expect to see the look of utter despair upon his face. She didn't know what to think and was afraid of what she might hear.

"So . . . you're home," she said.

Three small words. And the tone with which they were delivered made him shake. She sounded . . . she looked . . .

"You're mad at me," he said quietly. "I can tell. I always knew one day you would get mad at me for something. It's only reasonable to assume you would. I just never knew it would hurt so much when you did."

Tears sprang to her eyes. The quiet devastation in his voice was her undoing. She flew across the room and into his arms.

"Dear God, Joseph, I'm not mad. I'm scared. I've been imagining all sorts of things, like kiss-off speeches and Dear John letters and—"

"Just shut up and kiss me," Joseph begged. "I've been through hell. The only thing that kept me sane was the thought of you and Joey here, safe and waiting."

She tilted her head, slid her hands around his neck, and pulled him down to her waiting lips.

The touch was a mixture of hope and desperation. Of the need to hold and be held.

"Where's Joey?" he muttered when he came up for air.

"In bed asleep."

"Is he all right? She didn't do anything to him, did she? I was almost afraid to ask."

"He's fine, but you don't look so good. I think

you need a little of the same medicine I gave him."

"What—was he sick again?" A note of panic slipped into his question.

"No, just in great need of reassurance," she whispered. "But the dose I gave him will be too small for you. I think I'd better get you to your room. You don't look so good."

He began to smile. It was a heartwarming, soul-satisfying smile. "Does it hurt?" he asked.

"Not enough to notice," she whispered, and walked away, certain that he would follow.

"I wouldn't bet on that," he muttered, thinking how close he'd come to losing her today.

By the time the door had closed behind him, he had his shirt off, his belt undone, and was walking out of his shoes. A swift rasp of a zipper told Molly that there was no time left to waste. She stepped out of her shoes and unbuckled her belt, but it was the last thing she did as Joseph caught her from behind, scooped her into his arms, and deposited her onto his bed.

"I'm still dressed," she whispered, unable to take her eyes away from his body and the evidence of his desire for her.

"Not for long." He bent down.

As each garment was removed, he replaced it with a kiss. It took forever to get the job done, and by the time it was, Molly was in a fever of need and Joseph was blind with an ache that wouldn't stop.

The last bit of nylon and lace hit the floor as Joseph slid between her legs and into her body in one long, slow motion. But when he buried his face in the valley between her breasts, he groaned.

"I love you, Molly. Don't ever doubt that. Don't ever look at me again like you did today. I can't take it."

She barely heard his last four words, but they were enough to make tears come to her eyes.

"Don't doubt me," he begged. "I couldn't take that . . . not from you."

And then he began to move, and Molly lost all thoughts of answering. There was nothing but Joseph and his body, and his hands, and her heart keeping time with the motion.

Joseph felt the change in her body as it heated and then tightened around him. The blood rushed to his head, and then the heat inside him exploded, spiraling into one long gush. He lowered his head, captured the cry from her lips, and spilled himself into her.

"Well, Miss Jordan," the lawyer said. "I believe I understand your feelings, but whether the judge does or not remains to be seen. I've asked for a private hearing regarding the case soon. Until then, you're out on bond, and I'd advise you to make yourself available at a moment's notice."

Carly nodded and smiled, resisting the urge to slam the office door shut in his face. She stalked to her car while visions of diabolic retribution kept her from screaming.

She still couldn't believe what Joseph had done. He had actually stood aside and let the day-care center press charges against her. If she couldn't change his mind, she could be charged with kidnapping.

This wasn't what she'd planned. If she'd wanted out on the streets, she could have stayed in Natchez. At least there the police wouldn't have been after her. And then she remembered the hot checks and the angry wife—and those pictures she'd sent—and reconsidered her options. The police may very well *be* looking for her. It was possible that playing this episode low-key would be her best bet after all. Playing the injured mother wasn't quite her style.

She crawled into her car and for a few moments sat quietly to regroup. It was obvious that Joseph wasn't the easy nut to crack that she'd expected. And whoever this Molly Eden was, it was also obvious that the kid liked her a hell of a lot more than she'd expected. Carly shrugged. She couldn't help it and didn't really care. During her assembly, someone had left out the nurturing instinct, and she would be the first to admit that it was true.

"Okay," she muttered, "think, Carly. You can do better than this. What will you do—or better yet, where will you stay until this mess can be sorted out?"

And then a smile spread across her face. She started the car and pulled out into the traffic. If bluff didn't work, pity was next on the list.

The office door opened. Marjorie Weeks looked up and then blanched. Carly Jordan was back. And from the expression on her face, yesterday's meeting with her boss must not have gone as expected.

"May I help you?" she asked.

Carly teared, bit her lower lip, and wrung her hands before digging through her handbag for a tissue. She smiled at Marjorie through watery eyes and accepted the one that had been handed her.

"Thank you," Carly said, and then swallowed a dainty sob. "I don't suppose Joseph is in?" She knew damn good and well he wasn't. She'd been waiting outside in her car for over an hour, just watching for him to leave.

Marjorie shook her head.

"Oh, no." She sank into a chair, buried her face in her hands, and began to sob. "Then I don't know what I'm going to do."

Marjorie jumped to her feet. "Why, whatever is the matter?"

"Joseph and I used to be lovers." Carly managed a blush, playing her role of the injured party to the hilt. "We had a child, and foolishly I thought that Joseph could care for him better than I. I only wanted to see him," she cried, and allowed a fresh set of tears to flow.

"I don't understand," Marjorie said. Indignation for this woman's plight was growing. It was just as she'd expected. This poor woman was pining for her child.

"Yesterday I wasn't entirely truthful with you." Carly ducked her head, pretending to be embarrassed. "I tricked you into giving me the address to my child's day care. I just wanted to see him . . . to hold him. . . ." She moaned loudly and then blurted out the rest of her practiced recital. "Joseph had me arrested!"

"He didn't!" Marjorie couldn't believe her ears.

Carly nodded. "He claimed I was trying to steal Jody."

"Joey," Marjorie corrected.

Shit! Carly thought. *If this is going to work, I'll*

have to be more careful. "Joey," she repeated. "I just don't know what I'm going to do now. It took all my cash to get out of jail and now I have no place to stay."

Marjorie gawked. This was worse than she'd ever imagined. She couldn't believe that someone as kind and concerned a parent as Joseph Rossi could have the mother of his own son arrested. She fumed. It had to be that other woman's fault. She must have been jealous that the true love of Joseph's life had come back to reclaim her rightful place.

"Why . . . I can't believe my ears," Marjorie muttered. "What will you do . . . about the arrest and everything?"

Carly slumped. "I don't know." Once again, she managed a dainty sniff. "The hearing will be any day now. After I get this mess all cleared up, I'm just going to leave. I can't bear to go through this again." She cut her eyes up at Marjorie and then down at her lap. "If I only had a place to stay . . . at least until the hearing . . . then I'd be out of his life forever."

Marjorie heard herself say, "I suppose you could stay with me."

Somehow, the moment it came out, she had the distinct feeling that she should have kept her mouth shut. But, she reminded herself, it *was* her fault that Carly Jordan was in Oklahoma City. The least she could do was offer her a place to stay for a day or so.

"Why, that would be wonderful! You're just the sweetest thing!" And then Carly leaned forward and whispered. "But won't that get you in trouble with Joseph?"

Marjorie firmed her lips and stuck out her chin. "Not if he doesn't find out," she said shortly. "After all, I did nothing but offer you a room. I'm not actually getting involved in your business, you know."

Carly shook her head and then jumped up and threw her arms around Marjorie's neck. "You'll never know what this means to me," she cried.

And then the tears dried up too quickly to be believed. In the space of a heartbeat, she went from bawling to brisk and businesslike. "Now, if you don't mind, I could go on over to your place and unpack my things. Get out of sight before Joseph gets back, you know."

Although Marjorie nodded, she felt a little unsure. Things were getting out of her control. She dug in her purse, handed Carly her extra house key and the address, and as she did, realized that she'd just given a total stranger a key to her home.

"I'm sure things will work out," Marjorie said.

"I'll be home just after five. Please feel free to make yourself a sandwich if you get hungry."

Carly grinned. "You're a doll," she said. "I'll see you later," and with that, she left the office with her mission accomplished.

Marjorie sank back into her chair and watched the door slam shut. "Well!" she said to herself. "Well, now!" But there was little else to say. What was done was done.

Joseph, man that he was, wasn't aware of Marjorie's change in attitude toward him. She did her job competently and for him it was enough. It was Molly who felt the glares, the indignant expressions, and noticed the bitter twist to Marjorie's mouth. Granted, the woman had never seemed to approve of her, but this was so much more, it was almost palpable. She had no idea what had prompted this latest bit of disapproval, but she was certain that whatever had happened, Marjorie Weeks was ready to lay blame at her feet.

And it wasn't until the day of the hearing that Marjorie realized there was more to Carly Jordan's story than she'd been told.

Joseph slid the handful of papers into his briefcase, rolled up the drawings he'd been working on and slid them into a cardboard tube for safekeeping, then looked around his office to make sure he wasn't forgetting anything. Taking time off from work to attend this hearing was going to put him behind unless he finished the work at home tonight. He turned the light off in his office and then stopped at his secretary's desk on the way out.

"I'll be out the rest of the day."

Marjorie looked down her nose at him and sniffed. "Very well."

"If you need me, I'll be at the courthouse most of the afternoon. I have my pager."

The courthouse? Now he had her attention. Then that would explain her houseguest's nervousness this morning. Poor thing. She was probably scared to death. Although Carly Jordan had been at Marjorie's house only two days, she'd firmly insinuated herself into Marjorie's pity.

Intense curiosity overcame her good sense. The need to know what was going on overwhelmed her. "So you'll be at the courthouse."

Joseph nodded, then shoved his hands in his pockets and leaned against the desk, for the moment, postponing the inevitable. "Damn . . . I'm really dreading this."

"I can imagine," she muttered.

"I haven't said much to you about what happened the other day at Joey's day care, but it

203

hasn't been because I don't trust you. It's because it scared the hell out of me. I just couldn't bring myself to talk about it."

"Having to share parental responsibilities is probably difficult." She felt choked on the words as her deceit came home to roost.

"Share?" Joseph snorted. "If it hadn't been for me, there wouldn't have been a child at all."

Marjorie flushed. *Well! The absolute gall! The last I heard, it definitely took two to make a baby.*

"It could hardly have happened without her," Marjorie said primly.

Joseph grinned wryly, and then the smile disappeared. "That's not exactly what I meant. Yes . . . we made the baby. . . . Carly just didn't want to keep it. She planned an abortion without even considering my feelings. I talked her out of it with the promise that she'd have no responsibilities toward Joey again if she'd only carry him to full term."

She couldn't disguise the shock in her voice. "What are you saying? You can't mean she didn't want him?"

Joseph shrugged. "Hard to believe, isn't it? It was for me. Every day, every time I look at Joey, I think of how close I came to never knowing him." He frowned, then checked his watch. "I've got to hurry. I don't want to miss this hearing. There's no way Carly can be allowed to repeat this stunt again."

Marjorie could hardly ask, but something told her she must.

"I know it's none of my business, but exactly what did she do that was so awful . . . short of wanting to see the child, I mean?" She quickly added that last bit. In no way did she want her part in any of this known.

Joseph stopped at the doorway and turned. "She lied about who she was, pretended to be Molly, and simply walked away with my son, that's what."

"Oh!" Marjorie clasped her hand to her throat.

"See you later," Joseph said. "If I'm not back by five, just lock up. It'll mean I'm still in court."

She nodded. Speech was impossible. An awareness began to sink into Marjorie's consciousness. Something told her that there was a snake in the can of worms she'd opened when she'd sent that letter. The only problem was, she couldn't decide if she should stick that label on Carly Jordan or on herself.

Four hours and many tears later, Carly and Joseph walked out of the courtroom with their lawyers between them.

Joseph was disgusted but relieved, and didn't even acknowledge her existence as he shook hands with his lawyer and then walked away. Today was nothing more than a repeat of what he'd gone through when he'd gotten full and final custody of Joey to begin with, and no more than he should have expected.

The fact that at Joey's birth he'd had to officially adopt his own son because he and Carly Jordan weren't married had been one hurdle he'd overcome. The second hurdle had been that the courts couldn't quite get past the idea of a man capable of being a proper caretaker for a child, especially a child who was only days old. But to have to prove to a court that he loved Joey— when he'd been the only one who cared—had made him furious. Today was only a repeat of his frustration.

Carly's tearful pleas and promises had done exactly what she'd hoped. The judge had let her off with what he considered a stern warning about using other people's names under false pretenses, even though he understood her motives.

Joseph doubted that sincerely. Not even Carly understood what she was doing from one day to the next. And he still didn't believe she'd come out of motherly love. There had to be another reason. He just hoped to hell that whatever it was, she solved it somewhere besides the state of Oklahoma.

He slid behind the wheel of his car and headed

toward the day-care center. He'd had enough of courts and conniving women to last him a lifetime. All he wanted was to go home, spend a quiet evening with Joey, and consider himself lucky if Molly happened by.

Carly let her lawyer walk her to her car, smiling prettily up at him through a thick veil of tears, and then collapsed in his arms, sobbing heartily. Just when he'd begun to consider the consequences of personal involvement with a client, she pulled from his embrace, got into her car, waved, and drove away.

She was completely out of sight before he remembered she hadn't paid him the last half of his fee and that he had no permanent address for her.

He frowned and tried not to think that he might have been conned. It wouldn't do to let it get around that a lawyer had been had by one of his own clients.

Several blocks away, Carly smiled, tapping her freshly painted nails lightly on the steering wheel as she waited for the light to change. She was in a good mood. Everything had gone according to plan. Now if she would just hear from Enrique, she'd be out of here in a heartbeat and chalk all this up to bad judgment. Something had to happen soon. She had to be out of Marjorie's home before the first-of-the-month bills began to arrive.

She didn't think Joseph's secretary would be as sympathetic toward her when the phone bill came. As usual, Carly had made good use of a free ride.

She drove by the post office, checking, as always, to see if any mail had been forwarded to her in this city. She tossed the handful of bills in a trash can near the front door of the post office and then stopped in mid-toss as a long, thin envelope hung suspended between her thumb and forefinger. It had no return address, but the postmark was unmistakable.

It had to be from Enrique! She slit the flap with one long nail, then began to read.

Chiquita . . . imagine my surprise . . .

In the beginning, she held her breath. Halfway down the page she began to smile. By the time she reached the end, she was dancing in a circle, ignoring the curious stares and grins from the people inside the post office.

"Yes!" she shouted, and bolted for the car, her earlier frustration and anger forgotten as she began to compose her story. There was a phone number to call, and a promise of things to come that actually made her blush. "Good things do come to those who wait."

It didn't occur to her to wonder if Enrique Salazar would simply be using her for his own best interests and satisfaction. It never crossed her mind to worry about the future. As always, Carly Jordan lived for herself and the moment.

~ Nine

Carly paced the floor of her bedroom, afraid to come out and face Marjorie. After today, she could no longer pretend to be the injured party in this fiasco. She just had to figure out a way to postpone her eviction. After receiving Enrique's letter, his intentions concerning her were blatantly obvious. If there was one thing Carly was good at, it was recognizing opportunities. But making a grand exit at this point would be a trifle premature. All she needed was a little more time. And then she heard Marjorie coming down the hallway and frowned.

Oh damn, the old bitch is back.

Just for good measure she decided to try a rather loud sniffle and a muffled sob in the hopes that it would hold off the old girl—at least for the evening.

Marjorie paused outside the guest room door, imagining that she was witnessing the sounds of Carly's distress, and decided to give her the night to compose herself. But in the morning—that was another story. She'd been used and she knew it. Shaking her head, she walked away, wondering, again, how she'd ever let herself get involved in such a mess.

Carly paused in the middle of a sob, listening as the footsteps faded out of earshot, and smiled. It had worked. She dropped down into the middle of the bed and began filing her nails. If willing something to happen would make it so, then she should be out of here by the end of the week.

Molly paused in the act of emptying her dishwasher and stared at the calendar hanging near the phone. It had been years since she'd let herself remember this date. Although it wasn't snowing and sleeting as it had been all those years ago, it was still bitterly cold outside. Tears came without warning and she buried her face into her hands as she let herself think of the baby who'd died.

"Oh God, will this ever stop hurting?" she whispered, and tried to think of something else. But after knowing and loving Joey, it was impossible not to think of how much she'd missed when her own little girl had not survived.

She never saw a sunrise . . . or my face. I never heard her laugh . . . I never even heard her cry. Her presence in my life was so sweet . . . and too short.

Now, when she had so much to hope for, when another man's child had stolen her heart, she wondered if it would all come to nothing after all. The reappearance of Joey's natural mother had given her nightmares, and in spite of everything Joseph swore, she couldn't help remembering another woman with more claim to a man than she'd had. Joseph's call about the judge's decision had given them all cause to worry. Expecting Carly Jordan to wind up behind bars had been a little premature. Knowing that she was still out there—somewhere—seemed a persistent and ominous threat to everyone's peace of mind.

And while Molly didn't love Duncan anymore, and hadn't loved him since the day she'd learned of his deceit, the pain of rejection and the knowledge that she's been "the other woman" then, just as she was "the other woman" again was, in her mind, cause for great shame.

"I've got to get out of here," Molly muttered, and walked out of the kitchen, leaving the half-empty dishwasher and her troubles behind.

She paused at the hall closet and slipped on a jacket, dropped her house keys in the pocket, and walked out of the house and into the chill night air. She'd been inside too long alone with her thoughts. The more she thought of Joseph and Carly, the crazier she became. Joseph said it was over, so it was over. But she couldn't forget walking into the day-care center and seeing that woman all over Joseph like flies on butter. And she'd convinced herself that since yesterday's hearing, Joseph had been distant.

Maybe he's regretting his decision to press charges. Maybe the sight of Carly brought back memories he thought he'd forgot. He had said that when he and Carly were together he thought he'd never love anyone else. Maybe he was just fooling himself about hating her now.

"And maybe I need to get another life," Molly muttered. She passed a man on the sidewalk who was walking his dog, and she was instantly thankful for the cover of night. At least he wouldn't recognize a crazy woman who talked to herself in the dark.

The November air was sharp. She looked up at the stars, remembering how, as a child, she'd thought of night as something to be afraid of. Now, it was one of the few times in her life when she felt peace.

She liked her job. Everything in the florist business revolved around holidays and events. But she found that her life now revolved around her next-door neighbors. She tried to remember what it had been like before Joseph and couldn't. It seemed as if he and his son had always been in her life. Tears pricked the corners of her eyes as she tried to imagine life again without them.

Molly was in love. Hopelessly. But she wondered where they would go from here. She didn't always want to be Joseph's lover and Joey's friend. She wanted it all. The only question was, did Joseph want more?

Molly sighed. In her heart, she knew her earlier fears were nothing more than an overactive imagination. The disgust and rage on Joseph's face when he'd seen Carly had been too real to manufacture. He *did* hate Carly, with a passion. And he *did* want her out of their lives. It was just that after seeing Carly, and knowing what she was capable of, it was a wonder that Joseph had ever had the guts to trust another woman.

That was most of what was bothering her. What if he didn't? What if he managed to love, but not to trust? Without one, the other was impossible. He'd asked her to trust him. But was he capable of trusting her?

She kicked at a crack on the sidewalk and then stepped on it purposefully just to prove that she'd long ago gotten over that old childhood superstition. Yet as she walked, she knew that her mental wanderings were only postponing the obvious.

Face the facts, she told herself, and then groaned. *I would, if I only knew what they are.*

Granted, making love with Joseph was more than perfect, but he had yet to ask for more than her body. He'd said he loved her, but did he love her enough to spend the rest of his life with her? Molly turned the corner and saw the brightly lit sign of Braums Ice Cream store, which was her destination. Moments later, she started to cry.

"All he has to do is ask," she muttered, swiping angrily at the tears streaking down her cheeks. "Then I wouldn't be walking alone at night in forty-degree weather to go eat ice cream. I'd be with him—in bed—melting the damned stuff."

A car came up behind her. Lights flashed, and she heard a window being rolled down. In the dark, on a city street, she should have been scared out of her mind, but all it did was make her mad.

"Hey, baby," a male voice crooned, and then someone else in the car made a rude remark and laughed. "A pretty thing like you shouldn't be out alone on a night like this."

Molly turned and glared. "Don't think I don't know it," she yelled. "But what do men like you do when someone wants a commitment? Nothing! That's what! Absolutely nothing."

The smirk on the man's face slid sideways. He wasn't certain what had just happened, but he'd definitely lost control of the situation.

"You're all just alike," Molly yelled. "Beat it. I've been had once too often in my life. You're way the hell too late to do any more damage. Go pester someone else."

The window closed, the tires left rubber on the street as it shot away from the curb, and Molly threw her hands into the air and chastised herself through a mouthful of tears.

"What's the matter with me? I think I just insulted a mugger. I need that sugar fix worse than I thought."

She ran the rest of the way to the store, hit the door to Braums with the flat of her hand, and burst inside as if she were being chased.

"I want a dip of pineapple almond yogurt on a sugar cone," Molly said breathlessly.

"That bad, is it?" the waitress asked, eyeing Molly's disheveled appearance and the shortness of her breath.

Molly rolled her eyes and nodded. "Better make it a double."

The waitress laughed and went to fill the order. In her job she saw all kinds, and it took a lot more than one lone woman in need of sweet consolation to surprise her.

216

Minutes later Molly was nearing home, shivering as she licked the last bits of frozen yogurt from her fingers. She turned the corner, fixing her destination on the house next door instead of her own, ignoring the fact that it was nearly nine o'clock at night.

There was a light on in his study, so it was obvious that he was still up. And she wanted—no, needed—an answer to the question that kept haunting her.

She punched the doorbell with overzealous determination and waited on the front porch, licking her fingers between shivers. But when he opened the door, she forgot why she'd come. All she could do was wonder why men always looked so damn appealing in T-shirts and blue jeans.

"Molly! What in the world are you doing out here in the dark? Are you all right? Has something. . . . ?"

She pushed her way inside, jabbing a finger against his chest and ignoring the fact that she hadn't even said hello.

"I'd like to know something, Joseph Rossi," she said shortly.

His mouth dropped. That sharp poke against his T-shirt wasn't all that friendly. He wondered what he'd done now.

After the brisk night air, the room in which she

stood was suddenly smothering. Without think-ing, Molly unzipped her green jacket and then shoved her hands in the pockets of her blue jeans, unaware that it stretched the fabric of her soft cot-ton sweater too tightly across her breasts for Joseph's comfort. And if she had known, she wouldn't have cared. She'd managed to work herself up into a really good snit.

"You have something in your hair," Joseph said, and plucked the bit of brown crust out of a wayward curl stuck in the neck of her jacket. "It looks like—"

"Ice-cream cone," she said shortly. "Don't change the subject."

"I'm sorry," he said, grinning. "I don't know what the subject is."

"Yes . . . well," she said, suddenly realizing how foolish she must seem. "I guess you ought to know by now. . . ."

Joseph bent down. His lips grazed the pout of her lower lip just enough to taste. His tongue snaked out and slid across the curve once, twice. He groaned and lifted his head.

Molly forgot what she'd been about to say. She was lost in the dark fire of his gaze.

"Chocolate chip," she muttered.

"Tasted more like pineapple to me," Joseph whispered.

"No . . . I meant your eyes. They remind me of chocolate chips."

"Hell, honey, are you all right? You come in here mad, with ice-cream cone in your hair, pineapple on your lips, and chocolate on your mind? What's a man to think?"

Molly groaned. What had seemed like a good idea earlier, suddenly seemed foolish. "I think I'll leave now," she said, and headed for the door.

"Not so fast." Joseph grabbed her by the arm, tugging gently as he turned her to face him. He tilted her chin with the tip of his finger, gazing long and hard into those clear blue eyes, and tried not to smile. "I think you and I need to talk, my love."

Molly's face lit up. "Am I really?" she whispered, and slid her arms around his neck.

Again, she'd lost him. That answer didn't fit what he'd just said. He buried his face in the collar of her jacket, inhaling the scent of cold, fresh air still clinging to her hair, and smiled, remembering the bit of ice-cream cone.

"Molly, I think you should start over," Joseph said, and this time he couldn't stop the laughter.

She groaned, slid her arms around his waist, and knew that if she looked up, she would be blushing.

"Never mind," she whispered.

"Oh, no, you don't," he said, and shook her gently. "You don't get away with this so easily. You can't come barging in on me and accuse me of nothing. Not me, you don't. I don't take nothing sitting down."

She started to laugh. He was right. She had absolutely nothing to be mad at him about. Not really. She sighed, wondering if this evening was just an early sign of PMS.

"Oh, Joseph, I love you," she laughed, and then stopped short. She hadn't meant for that to come out—not exactly like that, and not here in the hallway of his house with ice cream all over her face.

The laughter in his eyes was replaced by a look that she'd come to know well.

"That's probably the best thing I've heard all day," he said softly.

He cupped her face in his hands then bent down, slowly. His mouth grazed the tip of her nose, "I . . ." then slipped to the left corner of her mouth, ". . . love," changed directions and moved to the right with startling accuracy, ". . . you," caught the surprised gasp coming out of her mouth by covering it with his own, ". . . too."

By the time the kiss had ended, Molly was completely devoid of traces of ice cream as well as makeup, and was contemplating a second trip

to Braums just to get her face washed like this
again.

"I think I've made my point," she whispered,
closed her eyes and stepped back from his embrace while she still had the strength to stand.

"You're leaving?" he mumbled, unable to think
past the ache she'd created and the fire that she'd
built.

"Good night, darling," she said softly, smiled
and waved, and shut the door behind her on her
way out.

Joseph stared blindly at the closed door and
wondered what the hell had just happened.
Whatever it was, it had left him in serious condition. Taking a second shower was suddenly the
uppermost thing on his mind. Long—and cold. It
was either that, or try to figure out what Molly'd
meant. He opted for the shower. It would be simpler than trying to figure out what went on in a
woman's mind.

For Carly, the morning had started off perfectly.
As if on cue, the call from Enrique that she'd been
waiting for had come while Marjorie was fixing
breakfast. Now she was tossing clothes into her
suitcase with wild abandon, gleefully dancing
from closet to bed and back again as she continued to pack. She could still see the curious look

on Marjorie's face when she'd handed her the phone.

"It's some man . . . for you," Marjorie said shortly. "How did he know to call you here?"

Carly simply smiled and shrugged, slipped the receiver to her ear and waved her thanks, indicating the need for privacy.

Marjorie left the room, but not so far away that she couldn't discern this call had been expected. She began to wonder what other surprises she might have in store.

"It serves me right," she muttered, and hurried off to finish dressing for work. "Next time, I swear I'll mind my own business."

She had no way of knowing that her guest would be gone when she returned that night. If she had, the day would have gone a whole lot faster.

Sure enough, Carly left the house only minutes behind Marjorie, and as the cab maneuvered the thick morning traffic, she did a mental count of her money and her good fortune. While she was a tad bit shy of the first, Carly felt herself more than compensated by her luck on the last.

When the cab pulled up at the terminal to Will Rogers Airport, Carly took a deep breath and resisted the urge to keep looking over her shoulder. She kept telling herself she was home free. But until her plane actually left the ground, she wouldn't feel safe. Visions of being stopped at the gate by plainclothes detectives had alternated with visions of angry ex-wives and unpaid bill collectors.

When her flight was called, she was the first in line. The pilot winked at her as she stepped on board, admiring her slender figure and elegant white two-piece suit.

Carly, being Carly, quickly accepted the innocent flirtation as her due. She took a seat by the window, buckled up even before it was time, and leaned back with a slow sigh of relief. She closed her eyes, ignoring the heavyset woman who took the seat beside her, and tried to concentrate on the best way to permanently insinuate herself into Enrique Salazar's life. Carly had already made up her mind that a "south of the border" address was to be her next destination.

A young woman came up the aisle carrying a small child in her arms, obviously struggling with excess baggage as well as the baby, and for a moment, Carly was reminded of what she was leaving behind. Just the thought of being in this woman's shoes made her ill. As the child began to cry, she looked at the woman with a mixture of pity and disgust and didn't bother to lower her voice as she remarked, "Oh, great. A squalling brat all the way to Baja."

The woman sitting beside her frowned, but the new mother didn't seem to mind. She simply slid her bags off her arms, letting the stewardess put them into the overhead rack, as she quickly seated herself and her baby to clear the aisle. Carly watched as the woman seemed to sigh with relief at being off her feet. As the young mother began surveying her surroundings and her seatmates, Carly thought about looking away before she was caught staring. But she didn't.

It was one of those moments in a person's lifetime when just for a second you connect with a stranger in an unexpected way, because the woman stared straight into Carly Jordan's eyes. Oddly, it was as if they could sense each other's thoughts. Carly's disgust. The weary patience of a mother running on empty.

And then the child settled, lying against his mother's breasts, and very slowly he slid his chubby little arms around her neck. In spite of his intention to remain alert, his little eyes fell shut.

As the child's exhaustion became obvious, his show of affection quickly took the mother's attention. She broke contact with Carly to look down upon her baby's face, smiling gently as she quietly kissed the tip of his nose.

The action was nothing Carly hadn't seen parents do a thousand times in her life. It had never affected her before, so she wasn't expecting the wash of emotions that almost overwhelmed her. For a second, the bond between that mother and child physically hurt her. She inhaled sharply, then looked away, staring instead out the tiny window onto the tarmac below.

When the plane began to move, she breathed a slow sigh of relief as the runway began to fade from view. Higher and higher the jet climbed into the air, and the farther she got from her past, the thicker the tears that blinded her vision. Blinking furiously, she focused her attention on the things that mattered, and furiously discarded the unwanted sentiment from her thoughts.

What the hell is wrong with me? When I get to Enrique, I'll have everything I've ever wanted.

And by the time drinks were being served, she'd convinced herself that it was true.

Marjorie came home to a short thank-you note and a blessedly quiet house. Her guest was gone.

"No saying where to, or who with," Marjorie muttered. "And she didn't leave my key. That settles it. I'm changing the locks."

But Carly Jordan's departure wasn't a shock. It was a welcome relief. For the first time since she'd sent that ill-fated letter, Marjorie slept like a log. And when she arrived at work the next day, even Joseph noticed her lighthearted attitude and the constant smile on her face.

"You're awfully chipper this morning," he said, as she handed him his mail.

Marjorie blushed. And then her conscience demanded that she at least share part of her news with him. After all, he would be the one most affected.

"I have a confession to make," she said. "I hope when I tell you that you'll understand. I never meant to get involved."

Joseph waited. Obviously something was weighing heavily on Marjorie's mind.

"The day after the incident at the day care, Miss Jordan came into the office looking for you." She flushed as she watched his mouth grow grim. "Now remember, you'd told me nothing of what had happened until much later."

Joseph nodded. "Go on."

"She came in all upset and crying, said she was searching for you. When I told her you were gone, she started crying even harder. I felt so sorry for her that before I knew it I heard myself offering her a place to stay until everything was sorted out."

"Good Lord! Do you mean to tell me that she's been staying at your house all this time?"

Marjorie looked away, unable to face him. He

was angry, she could just tell. She liked working here. She didn't want to look for another job, and at her age, they were harder and harder to find.

"I'm afraid so," Marjorie said. "Once she'd settled in, I didn't quite know how to get rid of her."

Joseph sighed, then relented. He knew all too well how Carly could work a person around to her way of thinking. He'd suffered it for years, but only because he thought he'd loved her. It was only later that he realized how shallow and selfish her actions really were.

"Look, I understand how things happen," he said. "But why are you so happy about it?"

Marjorie beamed. "Because she got a phone call yesterday. To make a long story short, she's gone. And I say, good riddance!"

And then she flushed, realizing that she'd just slightly slandered Joey's natural mother.

Joseph felt a tension beginning to ease from the inside out. It was as if a great weight he'd been carrying suddenly disappeared.

"Thanks for telling me, Marjorie. That's the best news I've had in weeks."

She preened, slipped back into the chair behind her desk, smoothed the high, gray crown of her perfectly lacquered hair, and felt vindicated for what she'd done. Granted, she hadn't told him everything. But there was no need. It was enough that she regretted it and knew that it would never happen again.

The days flew by, and before anyone thought it was possible, Thanksgiving had arrived.

A light dusting of snow almost covered the dry, brittle grass as Joseph and his son made their way across the lawn to the house next door. Their invitation to have Thanksgiving dinner with Molly had been welcome. Sitting down to a real family dinner would be a first for both father and son.

Joey ran in fits and jerks, flying off to see something that caught his eye and then dashing back to get his father to come look. By the time they arrived on Molly's doorstep and rang the bell, their faces were red from the cold, but their eyes were full of sparkle.

Molly opened the door and then laughed at the pair standing on her doorstep. Joseph looked ready for a warm fire, and Joey looked as if he'd just started to enjoy the freezing temperatures. She watched as Joey began to dig through a pot of snow on her front porch that had been overflowing with geraniums earlier in the year.

"Hey! Who is that digging in my flower pot?"

Joey looked up and grinned, delighted that Molly was already into a game.

"You know me," he answered.

Molly frowned and shook her head. "No . . . I don't believe I do," she said, then knelt, pretending to try to guess. She tweaked his red-chilled nose and then laughed. "I know who it is! It's Rudolph the red-nosed reindeer!"

Joey shrieked with joy. "No! It's me, Joey."

Joseph scooped him off his feet and dumped him inside Molly's front door.

"So, Joey, let's get inside before we let out all of Molly's heat."

From past experience, Molly knew that Joey would not be satisfied long with the small assortment of toys she'd slowly been accumulating, she had rented several Disney videos to allay any boredom. It took Joey no longer than thirty seconds to spy the tapes, and even less to wheedle an instant viewing of the first. Within minutes, Joseph had him settled in place, watching the antics of a young beggar boy who kept escaping from soldiers on a magic carpet.

Joseph paused in the middle of the room, eyeing his son one last time, and at the same instant taking note of the warm, homey atmosphere of Molly's house, the scent of roasting turkey, the yeasty smell of fresh bread, and an underlying blanket of sweet and spices, which he hoped spelled pumpkin pie.

How is it possible that one woman could make such

229

a difference in our lives? Suddenly, he wished he
never had to make the trip back across the yard to
his house, because this house felt different. This
house was a home.

"Happy Thanksgiving," Molly said, and laid
her head against his arm.

Joseph turned, took one look at the longing in
her eyes, and swept her into his arms.

"Happy Thanksgiving to you, too, sweetheart," he whispered, and tasted cinnamon on
her lips.

Well aware of his son only feet away, their moment was swift, but sweet. When he could think
without the room spinning at his feet, he cupped
her face in his hands and feathered one last kiss
across her brow.

"Everything smells wonderful," he said. "Want
some help?"

I want you. She smiled. "It depends," she
drawled. "If you promise not to taste more than
you chop, I could use some help with the salad."

Joseph gave Joey one last glance, just to make
sure he was still entranced with the movie, and
then took Molly by the hand.

"I'm your man," he said. "Just lead the way."

Oh, Joseph, if only you were my man. But Molly
wisely kept her wishes to herself and, as the day
progressed, pretended to herself that they were

truly one, big happy family. That she had every right to wash Joey's face, kiss his hurts, and make love to Joseph Rossi any damn time she pleased.

The next day brought them back to Molly's house to finish off the leftovers of yesterday's feast. In the midst of clearing the dining room table, she was forced to keep stepping over the two males rolling on her floor in a fierce mock wrestling match. She rolled her eyes. They had too much energy to be indoors, and with that, came an idea. She dumped the last of the dishes into the sink and then made an unexpected request.

"Let's go to the mall."

"Oh my gosh," Joseph groaned, and lifted Joey over his head to keep from being pummeled. He'd been trying to watch a football game and fend off his son's latest choke hold at the same time. "You feed me solid for two days and then expect me to go shopping? You've got to be kidding."

Molly grinned. "No, I'm not! It's tradition. The day after Thanksgiving is usually the busiest shopping day of the entire Christmas season, except for Christmas Eve."

Joseph groaned. "And this is the day you want to tackle the malls? You're kidding!"

She shook her head. "No, I'm not. Besides, if we go, Joey will get a chance to see Santa Claus."

Joseph started to smile. The method in her madness was becoming all too clear. She didn't want to shop. She wanted to watch Joey see Santa.

"Wanna see Santa," Joey shrieked.

Joseph ruffled his son's hair in a teasing manner. "You don't even remember Santa."

But Joseph lost and Molly won, and a few minutes later they were parking at Penn Square Mall amidst the barrage of early shoppers looking for bargains.

Only when it came time to sit in Santa's lap, Joey balked, and it was Molly who did the deed. Amid laughter from onlookers, Molly took her seat and smiled and waved at Joey, who'd gotten a sudden case of bashful.

"Ho, ho, ho!" Santa said, happy for the time being to have a pretty woman in his lap rather than a wiggling, crying child. "And what do you want for Christmas, little lady?" he asked.

Suddenly, the foolishness of it all was gone as Molly leaned over and whispered in the burly man's ear, unable to say aloud, even to a stranger, the wish dearest to her heart.

The smile beneath Santa's beard froze on his face. He looked at the woman on his lap, and then out across the crowd until he spied a tall, dark-haired man with a boy in his arms, and nodded, as if to himself.

"Santa will do his best, little lady," he said gently. "But that's a mighty tall order . . . even for me."

Molly smiled. "I have faith," she said.

"I'll say a prayer," he said solemnly.

Molly nodded, satisfied, and then made her exit. She was certain that she'd done all she could toward the situation at hand. For the moment, her life was in the hands of fate—and a fat man's prayers. It would be two days before Molly's life would change—in a way she would never have expected.

Molly downed the last of her coffee and glanced at the clock on her kitchen wall. She'd overslept and was going to be late for work. But her bed had been so warm, and it was so very cold outside that getting up and getting dressed had been the last thing on her mind.

Partly out of perversity, and partly from haste, she'd chosen an outfit she'd had for years. The blue turtleneck sweater was old but warm, and her navy wool slacks were the same. And if she got something on them at work, it wouldn't be the end of the world. It would simply give her a good excuse to buy a new outfit.

She dumped the coffee dregs in the garbage disposal, sloshed a little water in the cup, and then made a run for the front door. She had one arm in her coat and was struggling to catch the flight of the other when the phone rang.

"Darn," she muttered, and considered letting the answering machine pick it up. But manners won out, even though the caller didn't know she was here.

"Hello."

"Molly . . . thank God you're still home," Joseph mumbled.

Molly's heart skipped a beat. He sounded so strange.

"Are you all right?" she asked. "You don't sound so good."

Joseph sat back down on the side of the bed to keep the room from spinning. "I hate to ask you," he said. "But I need a favor. Could you come and get Joey, take him to day care for me, and then pick him up this evening? I don't feel so good. Maybe if I spend the day in bed, by evening I'll be ready to deal with him."

"I'll be right there," she said.

Moments later she burst through the door, dumping her coat on a chair in the living room, calling his name as she ran through the house.

"In here," he said, and then dropped his head back onto the pillow.

She didn't know what she expected, but this weak and pale man laid out on his bed was not it.

A sudden overwhelming need to cuddle him hit. But he was too big to lift, so she settled for a caress instead.

Her hand swept across his forehead, and then down the curve of his cheek. He was wearing old gray sweats, and the heat in the house had to be in the eighties, yet he shook with a chill.

"You have a fever and a chill. Get under the covers," she ordered. "Where's Joey?"

Joseph moaned as he crawled back between the sheets. "In his room playing, I think."

"I'll be right back," she said. But Joey wasn't in his room playing. He was dressed, but curled up in the middle of his bed, his face flushed, his thumb in his mouth with Thumper clutched tightly against his chest.

"Oh, honey," she said softly. "Are you sick, too?" She frowned, testing the hot, dry skin on his forehead.

"I sick," Joey repeated weakly.

"Don't worry," Molly said. "I'll take care of you." She stood up, uncertain of what to do first. And then she made a decision. "I'll be right back," she said. "Just lie still and hug Thumper so that he doesn't get sick, too, okay?"

Joey nodded and closed his eyes. Molly's heart jerked. He was too quiet and listless for her peace of mind. The Joey she knew stayed wired.

She hurried back into Joseph's room. "Joseph . . . sweetheart . . ."

He opened his eyes and tried not to groan. "What?" he muttered.

"Joey's sick, too. Did you guys eat anything last night that might have caused this? What did you have?"

It was the word "eat" that did it. Joseph rolled out of bed and into the bathroom just in time to keep from embarrassing himself.

Molly sighed and headed for the phone while Joseph washed his face and then dropped back into bed.

"Cora, I won't be in today," she said. "In fact, I'm not sure when I can make it. My two guys are sick, really sick. I don't know with what, but it's for certain that they can't be alone. I'll call you later, okay? Oh . . . and if you need extra help, you have my permission to call any of the temps in. It's about that time of year anyway."

She hung up, certain that Cora and Harry could do what was necessary to keep her business going. After all, she told herself, if the boss can't take a few days off, what good is it being the boss?

She had one more call to make, and glanced down at her watch as she made the call. Her old friend Dr. Marr was going to have to make another house call.

"Was it something they ate or something going around?" Molly asked.

Dr. Marr grinned. "Going around," he said. "Chicken pox. A real good case of them, too."

Molly gaped. Grown men didn't get chicken pox, did they? "Joseph, too?"

"Joseph, too. And, excuse my French, but his will probably make him sick as hell. Childhood diseases usually hit adults pretty hard." The doctor scratched his head and squinted his eyes as he considered their best course of action. "So, what's the scoop? Do I call an ambulance for the both of them, or leave it in your hands?"

"I'm staying," she said. "What do I do?"

The doctor nodded. He'd expected as much. He began to reel off a list of instructions that sent Molly scurrying for paper to write them all down.

"And don't hesitate to call if you can't handle them," he added.

She nodded as she let him out, and then shut the door. For a moment she let herself wilt. Chicken pox! She suspected that of the two, the father was going to be the biggest handful. And she was right.

"What the hell do you mean . . . chicken pox? I

237

can't have chicken pox. Only kids have chicken pox." Joseph's grumble coincided with a toss of the bedclothes away from his body.

Molly hid a slight smile, pulled a light sheet back up across his chest, and laid the cool cloth across Joseph's forehead, letting him complain about the inevitable.

"Well, you do. Both of you. And Dr. Marr said to stay quiet, drink lots of fluids, and above all . . . don't scratch."

"Hell," Joseph said weakly as he dug at a spot on his neck. Molly moved his hand, handed him the wet cloth, and went across the hall to get Joey out of his clothes and into pajamas. She had a feeling that the next few days were going to be long ones.

"Molly . . . call the office for me," Joseph called from across the hall. "Tell Marjorie I won't be in— and whatever you do, don't tell her why. I'll never hear the end of it. Chicken pox, for God's sake. Why couldn't I have just broken a leg or something? Tell her I'm . . . tell her we . . ." He groaned, coughed, and cursed.

Molly ignored his grumbles while she was tucking Joey back into bed. He, at least for the time being, was willing to sleep through his fever.

Moments later she was on the phone to her shop, explaining the situation to Cora and Harry, giving them instructions as to the orders they'd need to make for the week and Joseph's phone number just in case they needed further advice.

As she hung up, she rolled her eyes, trying to think of what she was going to say to Marjorie Weeks that would sound plausible and still not give Joseph's circumstances away.

"No use putting it off," she told herself, and made the call.

Marjorie answered on the third ring. "Red Earth Designs," she said.

"Marjorie . . . it's me . . . Molly," Molly said. She could imagine the freezing expression on the woman's face. For the life of her, she'd yet to please Marjorie, and this news wasn't going to help matters any. "Joseph asked me to tell you that he won't be in for a few days."

"A few days!" Marjorie couldn't keep the shock out of her voice. "But he has that consultation tomorrow . . . and a meeting with the Summers project the day after that. What'll I tell them?"

Molly sighed. "I don't know. Put them off, reschedule . . . do whatever it takes. He just won't be . . ."

From the corner of her eye, Molly saw a long shadow in the hallway and knew that one of her patients was out of pocket. Before she thought to cover the phone, she yelled aloud. "Joseph! Take that off and get back into bed." She'd seen him struggling with a jacket, trying to get his arm aligned with the sleeve.

Marjorie gasped. She'd already learned her lesson about interfering. But the very idea, carrying on like that with a small child in the house. What were they thinking? Couldn't they wait until she was off the phone?

Marjorie hung up in disgust.

Molly heard the sharp click in her ear and knew that what she'd said was probably being misconstrued. But she didn't have time to worry about that. From the look on his face, she knew she had to get Joseph back in bed before he dropped. If he fell, she'd never get him up off the floor.

"What are you doing out of bed?" she asked.

Joseph groaned. "I'm cold. I was getting my jacket."

"You don't put on more clothes in bed. You put on more covers," Molly muttered. "Come on, sweetheart, lie down. I'll get another quilt."

"She's calling me sweet names and I'm too sick to care," Joseph grumbled, more to himself than to her. But she heard him all the same and patted his back as she led him back to bed.

"It'll be okay," she said. "I'll say them again

when you're well. For now, please get back in bed."

He complied.

"Molly . . . my juice is all gone."

She groaned, rolled off the daybed in Joseph's office, and staggered down the hallway toward the kitchen. Thanks to Joseph's bellow, Joey was bound to wake, and then she'd never get that nap she needed so badly.

She poured a fresh glass of juice, swiping at a limp curl as she made a run for his room before he yelled again.

"Here you go," she said, trying to keep her voice down and not alert the child across the hall.

"Thanks," Joseph said, and absently picked at a scab on the end of his nose as he took the glass from her hand.

"Don't scratch," she said without feeling. She'd said it so many times the past few days, it had become an automatic order that came with no thought.

He sighed as he downed the juice, giving her a mournful look for thanks.

"If you itch too badly, I can always fix you an oatmeal bath," she offered, knowing full well that threat would be what it took to stop his marauding fingers.

241

"No!" he said, eyed her with something akin to venom, and dared her to argue.

She gave him a weary smirk and cocked an eyebrow as she left, just to remind him who was really in charge.

It was all she'd been able to do not to laugh aloud at the look on his face when she'd first suggested the baths. Explaining the medicinal effects of the oatmeal's starch on hot, itchy skin didn't help the fact that he'd been expected to sit in it while she sluiced him with the thin, soupy mix. Explaining that he couldn't do it himself because he couldn't reach all the places didn't help. What had finally done the trick was reminding him of the time he'd rescued her from the tub and the embarrassment she'd had to endure. She'd fixed his bath, but he'd taken it alone.

Joey, unlike his father, had taken to the idea with glee. He'd been fussy and demanding, just like Joseph, until she'd given him the bath. The relief from itching had been almost instantaneous. He'd liked it enough that whenever he was bored or cranky, the first thing he'd beg for was an "oatsmeal baff."

Molly suspected that she'd used more oatmeal in the last few days than the Forty-fifth Infantry used on summer maneuvers at Fort Sill.

Tiptoeing quietly down the hall, she returned

the glasses to the kitchen and then prayed that she'd have at least another hour of rest before Joey awoke from his nap.

Her head had barely touched the pillow when she heard him whimper.

"Want Momma," he said. And when Molly didn't appear instantly in the doorway, he began to cry.

She was down the hall in a flash. If he cried, he'd itch. And if he itched, he'd want another "oatsmeal baff," and she knew that her back would surely break if she had to lean over the tub again and wrestle a wiggly, itchy, nearly three-year old again.

"I'm coming," she called, and tried not to remember that it had been days since she'd had a full night's sleep. "Molly's coming, Joey. Don't cry."

Marjorie was incensed. Her boss's business was going to be in jeopardy if she didn't have some answers soon. She'd made every excuse she knew, but none had been satisfactory enough to ward off the most persistent of his clients.

She made a decision. She'd pick up that phone and call him and she'd do it now. There was no sense having to relay every message through that Eden woman.

"Why . . . she might not even be telling him I called," Marjorie told herself. She dialed and waited, frowning as she imagined the orgy she'd interrupt.

When the phone rang, Joseph and Joey were in bed together, listening while Molly read them a story. She dropped the book in her lap, stuck her thumb in the crease to hold her place, and reached for the phone.

Joey frowned, but Joseph wisely saw fit to distract him, knowing that it wouldn't take much at this late date to set Joey off. Frankly, he knew just how his son felt. He'd never been so out of sorts with the world in his entire life, and he was a grown man. He could imagine how frustrated Joey must feel, not fully understanding why he itched, and why he couldn't play outside.

"Hello," Molly said, and then mouthed to Joseph that it was his secretary. "Hi, Marjorie. Yes, Joseph's right here. I'll put him on."

Joseph glared. He knew that it would be at least two more days before enough scabs disappeared that he could make his way into society without revealing what he'd endured. Now he was going to have to think up excuses as to why he still wouldn't be coming to work.

"Hi, Marjorie, it's me. What's up?"

He rolled his eyes as he listened to her tirade of

complaints. "Well, just reschedule. That's all we can do. No . . . I won't be in tomorrow. I still . . ." Joey jumped right in the middle of his lap just as the word left his mouth.

"Oh my God," he gasped, rolled his son off his lap. "I've just been gelded."

In spite of her sympathy for his pain, Molly laughed aloud. It was impossible not to. Joey pouted at being ousted from his father's bed, and Marjorie Weeks turned three shades of red before she hung up the phone, ignoring the fact that she hadn't finished her complaints.

She couldn't believe what she'd just heard. They were actually doing it while she was talking to him on the phone. She buried her face in her hands and contemplated searching for another job. There was no way she'd ever be able to look Joseph Rossi in the face again, not after all this.

Joseph groaned, and then frowned at the look on Molly's face. "Don't laugh. You'll be the first one to suffer if this never works again." He lifted the covers just to check and make sure everything was still in place. "Thank God," he muttered. "I'm still all there. Joey . . ." He motioned for his son to crawl back in beside him. "Come here, son. Only this time, for pete's sake, sit still, okay?"

Joey nodded, crawled back into place, and

stuck his thumb in his mouth for assurance that at least something in his world still fit.

"Now . . . where was I?" Molly asked.

"The wolf was at the door," Joseph reminded her, very straight-faced. "He was huffing and puffing and . . ."

"Bowwed the house down," Joey shrieked and clapped.

Molly smiled. Like two peas in a pod, the Rossi men stared expectantly. Dark hair, black, dancing eyes, dimples, spots and all, they were hers. As weary as she was, she was blessed.

"Right," she said, ". . . and blew the house down."

She turned the page.

~ Ten

Marjorie Weeks had had enough. She was taking her concerns to the root of the problem. She'd left her last message, given her last excuse, and lied for the last time to Joseph's clients. She was going to talk to him face to face, and if that meant her job, so be it.

She stabbed the ON button on the answering machine with a perfectly manicured nail, as if daring it not to answer calls while she was gone, locked the office door, and headed for the parking lot. The wind was blowing, spitting snow and sleet into her face as she unlocked her car. But it didn't deter her from her plan. She would see for herself what was going on inside the Rossi house or know the reason why.

It didn't take her long to find Joseph's house,

but it did take her awhile to get up the nerve to park and go inside. She'd circled the block more than five times, and each time, she convinced herself that no matter what orgy she might interrupt, she was woman enough to bear it.

And then she remembered Molly shouting for Joseph to take off his clothes and get back into bed, and how Joseph had shouted and then groaned something about being emasculated, and she got red-faced just thinking about it.

Marjorie's ex-husband also received his fair share of unspoken curses as she continued to drive around the neighborhood, killing time until she got up the nerve to go to the house. She kept reminding herself that if he'd kept his britches zipped and his brain in gear, she would never have had to endure this latest bit of personal humiliation.

But self-pity was not Marjorie's strong suit, and she'd finally talked herself into a combative frame of mind. With a thrust of her chin and determination in her stride, she headed for the front door of Joseph's house with a "woe unto any who get in my way" expression.

Molly stared at herself in the mirror over the bathroom sink and tried to remember when she'd last put on makeup. There were dark shadows beneath her eyes instead of the powdered shadows she usually applied above. The only color on her face was a bit of something red that she suspected was strawberry jam from the sticky kiss Joey had given her minutes earlier.

It had been seven days—and seven sleepless nights—since Dr. Marr had diagnosed chicken pox. The Rossi men were nearly well. Molly, however, was a mess and running on empty.

"Oh God," she moaned, and shoved away from the mirror. "I could sleep for a year."

"Molly! Where are my gray sweats?"

Joseph's bellow echoed down the hall and into the bath off the kitchen. She stuck her tongue out in the general direction of his yell, and muttered under her breath, "Probably right where you left them yesterday."

"Molly!" he bellowed again.

"Coming," she shouted, and started toward his room when Joey came barreling down the hallway wearing his tricycle helmet and a pair of red pajamas.

"Joey, look out!" Molly dodged as the toddler nearly sideswiped her.

"Not Joey," he shouted, "I'm a Power Ranger," then hopped into a fighting stance and gave a fairly credible karate kick that landed him on his rear.

Molly would have laughed if her face hadn't

been too tired to change positions. Instead she stepped around the mighty mite and headed for Joseph's room.

"You shouted?" she asked.

He had the grace to flush. "I couldn't find my sweats."

That he was now wearing them was obvious. She eyed the soft gray fabric covering his long legs as well as the matching shirt dangling from his fingers. Her gaze swept across his bare brown chest, noting that nearly all signs of his spots were gone, and the few that were left were swiftly disappearing.

His hair was loose and a little shaggy around his ears, thanks to missing an appointed haircut, and the dimple on his cheek kept coming and going with regularity as he waited for her forgiveness.

"I'm sorry, honey," he said. "I guess calling for you has become a habit." His voice lowered, and his eyes darkened. "One to which I could very well become addicted."

Oh Joseph . . . if you only knew. I'm already hooked on the both of you. Please . . . please . . . please . . . don't let me go.

But he made no other declaration, and she managed a smile. Before she could aim their discussion into deeper territory, the doorbell rang and interrupted the moment.

"Door!" Joey shouted, and made a run across the hall.

But his bicycle helmet had slipped sideways, partially blocking his view, and he ran into the corner of the wall instead. It startled him more than it hurt, but when he hit the floor, he started to wail. Molly slid him out of his "magic helmet" and fished him up off the floor.

"Good gracious," she said. "I didn't think Power Rangers cried. They're too tough, right?"

He sniffed as the doorbell rang again, uncertain whether to succumb to self-pity or relate to the facts according to Molly.

Molly balanced him on one hip as she headed for the door. Rounding the corner as she entered the living room, she could feel the half-hitched ponytail she'd made of her hair coming down, and only then did she remember she still had not removed the jam kiss from her face.

She swung the door wide to find Marjorie Weeks on the front step, silently glaring, waiting to be admitted.

Oh, no, Molly thought. *She looks mad as an old wet hen.*

Joey wiggled on her hip, clutched a fistful of her hair, then buried his face against the curve of her neck and started to cry.

"Molly! Who is it?" Joseph bellowed from the back of the house.

For Molly, it was all too much.

"They've had the chicken pox," Molly said, and began to sob.

Marjorie took one look at the shadows beneath Molly's eyes, the tears flowing freely, the state of the house, the child in her arms, and knew that everything she'd ever thought about this woman had been unjust. She'd gone above and beyond the call of a next-door neighbor's duty.

"Here," she said shortly, ignoring Joey's wail. "Give him to me." She yanked the thumb from his mouth, kissed his cheek, and whispered the words "ice cream" into his ear. Startled by the unexpected offer of a treat so early in the day, he instantly hushed.

Joseph came into the room in time to see Marjorie yank Joey from Molly's arms. He was dumbstruck. What had happened to his Molly? She was crying.

"Now, now," Marjorie said, as Joey began to fidget. "In a minute, child. Right now, we'd better take care of Molly. She looks exhausted!" She fixed Molly with a steely gaze, daring her to argue with the authority she'd just usurped. "How long has it been since you slept?"

Molly sniffed, tried to remember and couldn't.

The tears came faster. "I can't remember," she sobbed, and sank weakly into a chair by the door.

"That's just what I thought," Marjorie said. "Here," she said, handing Joey to his father. "Go do something. Surely you have some ice cream or something that will pacify this child for a while. I've got to get this poor girl to bed."

Joseph stood openmouthed, his son in hand, and watched as his secretary hustled Molly out of the room. Although Marjorie had never been inside his house, she headed for his bedroom with unerring accuracy. Joseph didn't even pause to wonder how she knew where to go. There was nothing that woman ever did that surprised him.

And then it dawned on him that he should offer to help. He quickly settled Joey in the kitchen with some cookies and milk, and headed for his room. He could have saved himself the trip. Marjorie was posted at the door with a grim expression on her face that brooked no arguments.

"No, you don't," she said, as he started inside. "The poor girl is already asleep. What did you two do to her? I've never seen anyone so exhausted in my life!"

Guilt overwhelmed him. He hadn't realized how much she'd given of herself, and just for them.

"I didn't think . . ."

Marjorie huffed and rolled her eyes. "Men never do."

But she'd had her say. She rolled up her sleeves, eyed the clutter and dust, and headed for the kitchen. "Where's the vacuum?" she asked over her shoulder.

Joseph hastened to comply. He would swear later that he never knew what hit him. Before he'd realized it, Marjorie had set up a temporary office inside his home and had him returning calls and rescheduling appointments. He even found time to finish the drawings he'd started before he'd gotten sick.

"Silliest excuse I ever heard," she kept muttering, as she ran dust rag and child around the house. "Everyone has the chicken pox. It's no big deal. Men have no sense. No sense at all."

Joseph flushed, finally admitting to himself that his self-imposed quarantine had been motivated entirely from too much macho.

All sorts of guilt kept surfacing as Marjorie set the Rossi house back to rights. She couldn't help remembering what she'd imagined had been going on in here, and then comparing it with the actual events. Granted, she'd been wrong, but it hadn't happened often enough in her lifetime for her to be too concerned about the consequences. But what she was doing now wasn't wrong. She was fixing everything, and that was all that mattered.

"Do you think she's okay?" Joseph asked for the third time in two hours as he passed the door to his bedroom.

Marjorie nodded as she shooed him on by. "If she's already had the chicken pox, then the only thing wrong with her is she's exhausted. And"— she fixed him with a hard, pointed stare—"I'd better not catch anyone trying to wake her up. She's only been asleep six hours. The last I heard, she was behind seven days' worth. It'll take her a while. Go make some calls or draw something," she suggested, waving him away, "If I need you, I'll let you know."

"Yes, ma'am," Joseph said, and grinned, knowing when to leave well enough alone.

It was much later that night, when Marjorie had finally given up and gone home with a firm promise to be back early the next morning, that Joseph dared tiptoe into his own room.

He walked inside, looking at it from a much different perspective than the one he'd occupied for the last week. The room was dark, and looked much larger and less confining now that he wasn't tied to his bed by fever and lethargy. But his bed was another matter altogether. Molly was in it, and she looked so small and helpless it made him hurt. She'd wrapped herself into a ball and was sleeping so soundly that Joseph had to lean over and listen just to assure himself she was still breathing.

As if sensing his nearness, she stirred, then her mouth parted, and a small, nearly nonexistent sigh escaped. Her eyelids twitched, and a tiny muscle jerked at the corner of her lips. Joseph smiled gently. She was dreaming.

He knew Marjorie had gone home for the night, but he couldn't resist a glance over his shoulder, just to make sure, before he crawled into his bed.

Gently, so as not to awaken her, he slid his arm under Molly's head. She sighed and turned in his arms almost instantly, then threw a leg across his lower body, buried her face against the breadth of his chest, and settled.

Joseph's hold tightened in reflex, and then loosened almost as quickly. She was here—in his arms. She wasn't going anywhere. And as long as Molly loved him, neither was he.

Daylight came slowly, seeping beneath the space between the window shade and sill, sliding through and spilling down onto the floor like melted butter.

Molly watched, unwilling to move from the

warmth of Joseph's embrace. From the sounds of traffic on the street outside the house, she judged it to be well past 8:00. She'd lived in this neighborhood so long that she knew almost to the minute who was leaving for work, and in what car.

The neighbors across the street had a teenager who drove a car with a faulty muffler. He always overslept and waited until the last possible moment before leaving for school, gunning his engine as he roared down the street toward class.

The man in the house on the corner was fanatic about his morning ritual. He was always ready at least thirty minutes ahead of his wife, who also rode to work with him, and spent at least fifteen of those thirty minutes on their front porch yelling back into the house for her to hurry, that they were going to be late.

Knowing where one belonged was a comforting feeling and Molly knew good and well where she belonged: in Joseph's arms.

He moaned and then shifted, automatically pulling her closer against him as he resisted the urge his body clock was giving him to wake up.

Molly's heart caught, tugging at her conscience to remind her that all of this was still a conditional relationship. There'd been no declaration of anything more than love between them. She wanted more, much more. Molly wanted flowers and promises, some vows and a ring. She wanted forever.

Refusing, for the moment, to face the new day, she squeezed her eyes tighter and snuggled just the least bit closer against the curve of his lap. It felt so right to be held in this man's arms. And then a small, unexpected tear slid out the corner of her left eye and across the bridge of her nose, but she pretended it wasn't there. She wouldn't waste a moment in Joseph's arms with what-ifs.

Joseph lay quietly, feeling the change of tension as it came and went in her body. He knew she was awake. He'd felt her breathing change moments ago. It had almost been his undoing. Unaware of how closely they'd become attuned to each other's presence, he hadn't expected to feel the catch of muscles in her stomach as it contracted on a quiet sob. And when it had happened, it had been all he could do not to echo with a matching one of his own.

It was still a constant source of surprise to him that he'd let another woman get under his skin. After Carly Jordan, he'd been convinced that his trust of the female sex was all but dead. But that was before he'd been tempted by a woman from the Garden of Eden. He smiled to himself. If Eve had been anything like Molly, then it was no wonder the first Adam had met with a downfall.

His body stirred, a response to the warmth of her hips against the curve of his lap, and he was in the middle of considering the costs of starting something with Molly he might not be able to finish, when he heard sounds from across the hall. Joey was awake. He also knew, from experience, that it was not wise to linger abed and let him prowl the house alone. While Joey couldn't get outside—Joseph had long since taken care of that ever happening again—the kitchen and all that it offered was still fair game to an unsupervised child of nearly three. He groaned, planted a regretful kiss carefully in the middle of the tangle of Molly's curls resting just beneath his chin, and rolled out of bed.

The sweats that he'd slept in were only slightly wrinkled and none the worse for wear. He scratched at a lingering scab on his neck as he went in search of his son.

The few remaining spots he had were little more than dry, itchy places. Joey's had disappeared earlier, probably because of the constant oatmeal baths that he'd oddly adored. There was nothing for Joseph to do but get back to work—and that meant calling Marjorie and heading her off at the pass before she reappeared and began rearranging the rest of his life.

He entered the kitchen and caught Joey in the

midst of climbing onto a cabinet to get to the cereal. "Hey, buddy, where's my morning hug?"

The cereal was momentarily forgotten as Joey jumped off the cabinet and into his father's waiting arms.

A few minutes later, Marjorie Weeks rang the doorbell, and Joseph smiled as he let her in the house, stifling a sigh as he closed the door behind her. He'd forgotten to make that call. He followed her into the kitchen like a whipped pup.

"How is she?" Marjorie asked, swiping at a spilled milk on the table with one hand, and yanking Joey's thumb from his mouth with the other.

Joseph grinned. "She's fine . . . still asleep, I think. I was trying to get this guy fed without too much noise. I think I'll take him to day care today and try to get back to the office."

Marjorie frowned, hating to give up the tenuous toehold she'd made into this trio's life.

"I don't know, you wouldn't want him to overdo and have a relapse," she warned, all the while wondering how a child could have such an angelic smile and so many small devils dancing in those dark brown eyes.

"Dr. Marr called yesterday," Joseph said. "He's already given the go-ahead. And believe me, if I have to stay cooped up in this house another day with him, I'll be the one having the relapse." He ruffled Joey's hair and then smiled as Marjorie absently smoothed what he'd done to it back in place.

"You're the boss," Marjorie said. "I'll see you at the office later." With a regretful glance back at the pair standing hand in hand in the kitchen door, she waved and left.

Joseph waited until he heard her car leave the driveway. Only then did he breathe a sigh of relief. But Joey seemed to feel differently about his secretary's absence. He wore a frown beneath the remnants of his cereal. Joseph knelt down until he and his son were nose to nose, heads butting, and tickled Joey's stomach playfully as he spoke.

"I think you have a new champion," he said. "Mrs. Weeks seems to like you a lot."

"Nanny," Joey said succinctly.

Joseph had no words for his shock. His mouth quirked at the corner, and he tried desperately not to laugh. It would seem that his secretary and his son had shared a lot more yesterday than he'd been aware of.

"Nanny, hunh?" he said, and pretended to fall backward as Joey punched him on the shoulder in a mock-tough blow. He grabbed him and, together, they rolled over and over across the kitchen floor, ignoring the dry bits of sugarcoated cereal that caught in their clothes and hair.

Molly stood in the doorway, watching the hilarity unobserved, and when her heart hurt too much to breathe, she slipped back into bed, pulled the covers over her head, and pretended to sleep.

Unaware of being observed, Joseph managed to dress himself as well as Joey without making too much commotion. Certain that he'd accomplished a miracle by leaving her asleep, he left for work, leaving behind nothing of their presence but the crushed remnants of cereal on the gray tile floor.

Molly heard them pull away, and only then did she crawl out of bed and into her clothes. For the first time in over a week, she walked out of his house and across the lawn toward her own. There was a heavy frost from the night before, and the grass crunched beneath her feet. She blinked and sniffed, blaming her runny nose on the sharp, cold wind blowing in her face and not on the growing pain inside her chest.

Joseph slammed the phone down in disgust, aware that for the past two days, the only contact that he and Molly'd had with each other was through their answering machines.

He knew that Christmas was one of the busiest seasons at her florist shop. And Molly knew that because of being sick, Joseph was so far behind in his own work that he carried it home each night in an effort to catch up.

Nearly a week had passed since he'd returned to the office, and in that time, he'd felt Molly pulling away from the center of his life. Each time he'd broach the subject of her coming over, she seemed to have a reason for postponing the visit. There was a distance between them that hadn't been there, and he was beginning to think that while they'd been ill, Molly had gotten sick of their demands, that she no longer wanted to be a part of their lives.

It was his secretary who finally brought things to a head and made him reassess his earlier conclusions.

"I haven't seen your Molly in days," she said, as she laid a sheaf of letters on his desk to be signed.

"Neither have I," he said, and then shrugged. "Busy season and all that, I suppose."

Marjorie snorted. "No one is that busy," she said. "Did you thank her for taking care of you and Joey—like sending flowers, or candy or such?"

Joseph flushed. It had never occurred to him to do anything so formal as that.

He shrugged. "No . . . I didn't think . . ."

Marjorie threw her hands into the air. "Men never do. If you don't mind my saying so," she said, not waiting to hear if he minded or not, "I think something along those lines would be appropriate. Of course, flowers might not be the thing. Sending flowers to a florist is a bit redundant. You might consider . . ."

Joseph held up his hands in surrender. He recognized the look on his secretary's face. "I get the message," he said.

"I'll baby-sit, if needed," she offered, and bustled out of the room before he could argue.

Joseph couldn't wipe the smile off his face. Leaving Mississippi had possibly been the smartest thing he'd done in years. Once in his life he'd had no one. And now he was as near to a ready-made family as a man could ever hope to get.

But there was something he needed to do before he got down to the business of begging Molly's forgiveness. There was some old business in his life that needed to be put away for good. He wanted the business of Carly Jordan out of their lives forever.

He hit the button on the intercom. "Marjorie . . . get my travel agent on the phone. Book me a flight to Natchez, Mississippi, as soon as possible. I've got some business to tend to, and I want it over and done with before the holidays."

Marjorie smiled. "Yes, sir," she said. "And do you want me to make an appointment with your lawyer in Natchez while I'm at it—just in case he's planning to take off early for Christmas?"

Oh Lord, Joseph thought, *she reads minds, too.* "Yes, please," he said. "The number is on my—"

"I have it right here," she said.

"Of course you do," he muttered. "What was I thinking?" He hung up and then started to laugh.

Natchez had not changed, nor had his lawyer's attitude toward Joey's natural mother.

"My God!" Travis Marley said. "I knew she was off the wall, but I never thought she'd pull something like that. Whatever was Carly thinking? Hasn't she ever heard of parental kidnapping?"

Joseph shrugged. His lawyer had reacted just as he'd supposed, but it did nothing to stop the worry he'd been living with. He still had nightmares of Carly swooping down and spiriting Joey away again without his consent. It was why he'd come back to his hometown so suddenly, and to the lawyer who'd seen him through the trauma of trying to lay legal claim to his own son.

"I don't think Carly thinks, that's what I think," Joseph said.

Travis grinned. "What's that supposed to mean?"

"It means that I'm frustrated, and worried as hell. You're the lawyer. You tell me. What can I do to make sure that this doesn't happen again? Tell me something good. I didn't come all the way to Mississippi just to hear myself talk."

"Well . . . I can tell you this much. Carly Jordan is up to her ears in debt here. She skipped out on a lot of unpaid bills, and from what I hear in the courts, if she shows her face in town again, she'll wind up as correspondent in a very, very messy divorce. From what you've told me, I don't think you were anything to her but a port in a storm."

Joseph sank into the chair opposite Travis's desk and felt a bubble of tension slowly dissipating.

"Thank God! I should have suspected something like this. I couldn't imagine what on earth would have made her change. The woman I knew would eat her young. The Carly who showed up in Oklahoma City, swearing undying love and devotion to the both of us, didn't quite fit."

His expression darkened, remembering another time in his life and the devastation of finding out that the woman he thought he loved had existed only in his mind.

Travis nodded in agreement. "I'll file the information you gave me with the rest of your papers just to keep your file updated on the situation.

But I hardly think you'll be seeing anything of her again. Rumor has it that she's gone south . . . and I do mean south, as in . . . of the border. I hear she's gone on to bigger and richer things."

"I hope he has an iron constitution, a taste for barracuda, and a lock on his safe," Joseph drawled.

Travis laughed and stood as Joseph shook his hand. "Have a safe flight home, and invite me to the wedding."

Joseph grinned. It hadn't taken Travis long to read between the lines of his concerns.

"I've got to ask her first," he said.

The door flew open and Joey burst through, running, then jumping, into his father's out-stretched arms.

"Sorry," Travis's secretary said. "I hope you two were through discussing business, because your son is through with me."

Joseph laughed. "We were, and thanks again for watching him while we talked." He turned back to his lawyer and grinned. The dimple that Molly loved so much came and went at the side of his cheek. "I'll let you know about the wedding later. Right now, we've got a flight to catch, and then a woman to see about the rest of her life."

Molly hung up the phone and tried not to cry. Marjorie's message wasn't exactly what she'd expected to hear. Granted, she'd been slow about confronting her own feelings regarding Joseph. But she'd never imagined that he'd do anything so rash as leave the state without telling her, especially after all they'd been to each other.

It never occurred to Molly that she was the single reason he'd gone. Joseph was bound and determined that Molly Eden would never have cause to doubt him again. And the only way he knew to insure that was to make sure that his past was past tense.

"Okay," Molly told herself, "don't make a big deal out of anything until the roof falls in. I didn't exactly give him a golden opportunity to let me know he was leaving. It could be any number of things that sent him back to Mississippi. I don't believe for a minute that any of them have Carly Jordan's name on it."

"Did you say something?" Cora asked.

Molly made a face and tried to laugh. "Nothing worth repeating. I'm just feeling sorry for myself, and from the looks of these orders, I don't even have time to do that."

Cora grinned. "He'll come around. I know men, and that neighbor of yours is true blue all the way. Here, grab that pot of poinsettias and I'll get the other. We've got places to go and flowers to peddle."

Molly hugged Cora. "I don't know what I'd do without you and Harry."

Although pleased to hear the compliment, Cora was unaccustomed to so much sentimentality. She flushed, then smoothed her flyaway hair, yanked at her smock, and flipped a bit of wet leaf off the knee of her pants. "You'll do just fine, girl," she said. "You wait and see. I have a real good feeling about your Joseph . . . a real good feeling, indeed."

Oooh, Molly thought, *he gives me real good feelings, too*. And then wished she'd kept her memories to herself. She didn't have time to dwell on men, and love, and making love. Not even if hers had chocolate-chip eyes and shy dimples and made love with perfect passion.

∽ Eleven

Joseph stood at his bedroom window, watching as Molly unlocked her car and slid behind the steering wheel. He hadn't missed the number of longing glances she'd sent toward his house. Even from here he could see her frown. Regret for what he'd put her through overwhelmed him. But he had a plan, and nothing—absolutely nothing—was going to deter him from seeing it through.

He stepped away from the window before she saw him watching her, although the urge to dash outside and drag her into his house and into his bed was strong. At this point, he didn't think caveman tactics would get him far, and with Molly, he wanted to go all the way.

Joey came dawdling from the back of the house, dragging his Barney backpack along the floor. "Come on, kid, you're going to be late for day care and miss your morning snack. You don't want daddy to be late today, either." He scooped Joey up into his arms. "I think it's time to go find your momma."

Joey frowned. "Found my momma," he said, slammed his thumb in his mouth, and wiggled to be put down.

"Yes, you sure did," Joseph said, grinning as he kissed his son's soft cheek. "And we've got to hurry before someone else takes her. You found her, all right, but it's going to take a lot of sweet-talking on my part before she lets us keep her. Especially after what we put her through."

Joseph smiled to himself as he buckled his son in his car seat and then slid behind the wheel. He backed from his drive, easing carefully onto the main drag, always with one eye on the traffic and the other on his precious cargo. At a stop light, he fidgeted, anxious for it to turn green. He could hardly wait to start his day.

Molly twisted the piece of floral wire around the handful of ribbon she held looped in her hand, then fluffed it and stuffed it into the centerpiece she'd been working on for over an hour.

It was a vivid assortment of fresh greenery, holiday pine, holly berries, and Christmas poinsettia.

But the pleasure she would normally derive from creating such a masterpiece was gone. All she could think of was the last time she'd lain in Joseph Rossi's arms, and the way his mouth had fit precisely across her lips, and her breasts. She shivered and bit her lip to keep from groaning aloud.

The scissors she was holding fell to the floor with a clank.

"Cramps?" Cora asked, thinking that Molly's fingers had finally given out as hers had done hours ago.

Yes, but only of the heart, Molly thought. "Just clumsy, and a little bit tired." She glanced at the clock. "And it's only 9:30 in the morning."

Cora smiled. "If you're already watching the clock, I know you're tired. Buck up, here comes a customer. You take him. I'll finish this centerpiece."

Molly nodded and headed for the counter, wiping the bits of Styrofoam from her hands as she went.

"May I help you?" Molly asked.

The young man glanced down at his clipboard to check the name. "Is there a Molly Eden here? I have a delivery for her."

"I'm Molly Eden. Where do I sign?"

"Right here." The messenger handed her a small, square box wrapped in green paper.

Moments later, the bell over the door signaled his departure, but Molly was too busy tearing into the package to notice his exit. She opened the lid, tearing through the matching green tissue paper, and then stared open-mouthed at what was inside. Even from here she could smell the crisp, sweet scent of the dark red fruit.

"What is it?" Cora asked, and leaned over Molly's shoulder to snoop.

"An apple!" Molly turned the box upside down and shook it, expecting a card to fall out. But nothing did. There was no way to tell who the odd gift was from.

Cora frowned. "Who's it from? Be careful . . . don't bite into it until you check."

Molly shrugged, then grinned. "For what? Worms?"

Harry came sauntering in from the back room where he'd been unloading a new shipment of plants. He saw the women staring into the small box in Molly's hands.

"What's going on?"

"Someone sent Molly an apple," Cora said.

Harry shoved his cap to the back of his head and grinned. "Someone sent an apple to the Garden of Eden? That's a hoot!"

The light dawned. Molly began to wonder. *Could he . . . would he?*

She carried it, and the box, into her office, set the apple in the center of her desk, and then stood back, trying to imagine what message lay behind this unexpected delivery.

It was fairly large as apples go, and so shiny a red that Molly knew it must have been polished. The stem was intact, as if someone had just plucked it from the tree. She smiled, letting her imagination run free as she pictured Joseph reaching up, pulling it from the branch, and then turning to her with a smile on his face and the apple in his hand.

In her mind, she watched his even, white teeth bite down, saw the juice run from the apple onto his lips, and then shuddered as his tongue snaked out and caught the drip before it escaped. He chewed, swallowed, and then with a slow, sensuous smile, leaned forward and at the very spot where he'd taken the bite only moments before, touched the apple to her lips.

Molly closed her eyes, opened her mouth, and then let out a little squeal as the phone's loud ring startled her reverie.

"Oh my goodness," she gasped, and leaned against the desk. "I've got to get back to work. I must be losing my mind. I don't have time for daydreams of sexy men and apple juice."

Time and the telephone soon had her back at work, vivid reminders that the business of loving would have to wait for the business at hand.

Two hours later another messenger arrived with another delivery, and this time, Cora and Harry stopped what they were doing just to watch Molly's face as she began unwrapping the second box.

"What do you suppose it is?" Cora asked, pushing her husband aside none too gently in an effort to get a better look.

Molly's hands shook and her heart pounded as she quickly tore into the gilt-colored wrappings. The box was small, flat and narrow, and she couldn't imagine what . . .

"Oh!"

Her gasp said it all. The long fluorescent bulbs from the ceiling overhead caught the glimmer of gold as Molly lifted the delicate chain from the satin interior of the jeweler's box.

"Why . . . it's a necklace," Cora said. "And what's that little charm on the. . . . ?"

"It's an apple," Molly said, unable to wipe the silly smile from her face. "It's definitely another apple."

"But it's gold!" Cora shrieked, turning it toward the light.

Harry nodded, grinning sagely as he stuffed his hands in his pockets and sauntered away. "I told you someone was sending apples to the Garden of Eden. When I'm right, I'm right, by gum."

Cora rolled her eyes. "We'll never hear the end of this," she warned. "Harry worries a subject to death, you know."

Molly didn't care. If this meant what she hoped it meant, Harry could be right forever. She undid the tiny clasp and fastened the necklace around her neck, then pulled gently until the miniature apple was exactly in the middle of the long, gold chain and very, very, close to her heart.

Now work was impossible. Whenever a customer came in, everyone stopped what they were doing just to make certain that it was truly a patron and not another delivery in progress.

Lunch time came and went. The phone continued to ring, and they got so busy they let down their guard. That was why they didn't see the man until he came in the door. And they didn't actually see the man . . . only what he was carrying. All six feet plus of trunk and skinny limbs minus their leaves.

"Delivery for Molly Eden," the man said. "Where do you want it?"

Molly handed a porcelain reindeer to her customer and started to grin.

"What is it?" she asked, eyeing the heavy pot and the tall, skinny trunk of the tree he was carrying.

He leaned down, fingering the tag, then straightened and looked around curiously at the abundance of flowering things inside this shop and shrugged.

"Someone sent you a tree, lady. Not much of a present for a florist, but nevertheless, it's a tree."

Harry hooted from the doorway and slapped his leg, shaking his head with laughter as he helped a customer carry an armload of poinsettias to her car. "I'll bet it's an apple tree," he yelled over his shoulder.

The messenger looked startled. "How did he know?"

Molly grinned again, unable to stop the smile from spreading. "Is it really?" she asked.

"Says right here," the messenger said. "It's a Red Delicious."

"Of course," Cora smirked, eyeing Molly's auburn hair. "What else would it be?"

The customers inside the store began to grin, uncertain of the implications, yet positive that they were being let in on a very good joke on Molly.

"Oh, my!" Molly said, and blinked, surprised by the gush of tears that threatened to fall. She couldn't be crying in front of her customers, not even if it was from joy.

"No card—am I right?" Cora asked.

Molly could only nod.

It was 3:00.

The Garden of Eden was full of last-minute shoppers who'd left their own jobs just in the nick of time to visit the shop before Molly closed for the day. In honor of the holiday season, she always stayed open an hour later than usual, just for her working customers' convenience.

Answering phones and questions and ringing up sales, she was too busy to notice the bright pink van in the act of parking in front of her store. Had she looked, the multihued name, FANTASY MESSAGES, painted on the vehicle's side doors, would have been a hint of what was to come.

Also, had she looked up in time, she would have seen, along with her staring customers, a man dressed as a large green snake who was trying to make a professional entrance into the store while carrying a basket of apples. It was impossible. His tail kept getting caught in the door.

What she did notice was the sudden silence and then a couple of snickers from the corner of the room. She looked up and then gasped as the man wiggle-walked toward her, trying to alternate the swing of his tail with the scoot of his feet.

"Delivery for Misssss Molly Eden," he hissed.

Molly's grin was a bit lopsided as she stared at the basket of bright red apples he was carrying.

"That's her," Cora shouted, pointing at Molly. She couldn't resist a giggle. This was too good to be true.

The customers were surprised, but obviously enjoying the stunt at Molly's expense.

The messenger set the basket of apples at Molly's feet and began hissing his recital.

"I've been sssent to the Garden of Eden, to tempt a pretty misss. If thisss basssket of applesss doesssn't do the trick, then clossse your eyesss and turn around. Temptation behind you doesss abound."

Molly turned, her face a study in shocked delight. Joseph was standing behind her with an invitation in his eyes she couldn't turn down.

"Hi, honey. I miss you like crazy."

Between those dimples and his smile, he was irresistible. Seconds later, she was in his arms.

The hug he gave her was desperate as he closed his eyes and inhaled the essence of Molly, oblivious to the crowd of giggling customers around them.

"Are you still mad at me?" he whispered, and feathered kisses across her forehead and down the curve of her cheek.

"I wasn't ever mad."

"Do you forgive me anyway?" he persisted.

"Oh, yesssss," she whispered.

Joseph grinned. The snake had definitely done the trick. He watched over her shoulder as the man picked up his tail and slithered away as best he could.

Harry wasn't surprised by the turn of events. He'd known it all along.

The doorbell rang again, and Molly jerked, then spun, afraid to turn her back on that door again today. She smiled in delight at the sight of the pair who entered.

"Momma!" Joey pulled away from Marjorie Weeks's firm grasp and ran across the room. Customers were grinning broadly. Whatever was going on kept getting better and better.

Molly leaned down and caught him on the run, lifting him in her arms and savoring the kiss he planted on her cheek.

"Saw a snake," Joey shouted, pointing over his shoulder toward the door.

"Me, too," Molly said, and snuggled her nose against his ear, inhaling the sweet smell of child and cold air all at once.

"Get down, child, Molly's busy."

Marjorie's words were sharp, but her touch was gentle as she took the child from Molly and set him on the floor.

"Nanny . . . want an apple," he begged, pointing down to the basket of bright red fruit.

Molly grinned at the sheepish look on Joseph's face.

"Nanny?"

Marjorie flushed lightly as she handed Joey an apple.

"Well . . . the poor thing," she said, looking down at the child. "No mother, no grandmother . . . at least one of the Rossi men has some sense." She stared pointedly at her boss. "Unlike some I know."

Joseph rolled his eyes. "I'm doing my best in crowded surroundings."

"We'll see you later," Marjorie said. "At the house," she explained, extending the explanation to include Molly. "For the celebration dinner," she continued.

Joseph groaned, grabbed Molly's hand and headed toward the back of the building with her. Marjorie seemed determined to give away all his surprises. Before anyone could comment, they'd disappeared behind closed door. He took the phone off the hook and locked the door.

"I love you, Molly Eden."

Tears came without warning, blurring her vision and hovering at the edge of her eyes as she waited for him to continue.

"I know we've taken abominable advantage of you, darling, but we didn't mean to. I should have realized how exhausted you were."

Molly slid her arms around his waist.

"I'm not tired now," she whispered. "I think I'm ready, Joseph."

The smile slid off his face. The implications of what she was saying hit him full force.

"Ready for what?" he asked, unable to believe that she meant what he thought she meant.

"To be tempted," she whispered.

He groaned, lifted her off her feet and into his arms. "Molly, this is hardly the place, but I have this sudden, desperate urge to make love to you."

She had great satisfaction in knowing she'd struck a nerve when she saw his eyes turn black and his nostrils flare.

"The feeling is mutual," she whispered, and settled for the kiss he raked across her mouth.

Just before emotions got out of hand, Joseph remembered why he'd come.

"I don't have any more apples, sweetheart, and I'm fresh out of temptation—but I've got a lifetime of promises I swear that I'll keep, and it's all yours if you want it. All it takes is one promise from you."

Molly threaded her fingers through his hair and felt his body responding to her nearness.

"I'll promise you anything, Joseph Rossi," she whispered.

"Even promise to marry me?" he asked. He held his breath, waiting for the words that would make his life perfect.

Her tears spilled swiftly, but they didn't beat the smile on her face.

"I promise," she said softly. "It would be my pleasure—and I thought you'd never ask."

Joseph sighed and wrapped her in his arms. "I was afraid to," he muttered.

"Why on earth would you be afraid? You know that I love you. I've said it often enough to make a total fool of myself."

Joseph groaned, then cupped her face with his hands as he gently kissed her lips over and over between breaths.

"But I come with a hell of a lot of baggage, Molly. I have a past that I hope, but can't promise, will stay buried." He was referring to Carly, and they both knew it. "I have a child—and I think, as of last week, a ready-made grandmother—who'll demand their space in our lives."

Molly smiled through tears. She'd heard Joey

call Marjorie Nanny. It was fine with her. As far as she was concerned, there was no such thing as not enough love to go around.

"It sounds almost perfect," Molly said. "How could a girl resist such an offer?"

Joseph frowned. "Almost perfect?"

Molly turned away. The pain in her heart was almost too sharp to share. And yet if she and Joseph had a chance, there could be no secrets between them.

"I can't give you any more children, Joseph. Are you willing to settle for me . . . and less?"

"Oh, hell." The shadows in her eyes made him sick. He hugged her close. "How can you think that would make a difference to me? We already have Joey. And I do mean *we*. Remember, Joey's already staked his claim on you. It was left up to me to finish the job."

Molly shivered, then smiled through a fresh set of tears. She would have given a year of her life to be able to have Joseph Rossi's child.

"Damn it, Molly, don't cry," Joseph said. "I swear to God, somewhere there's a child being born, maybe today, maybe next year, but it has our name on it. We'll adopt a dozen if it'll make you happy. Remember, I know only too well how desperate a lad can be, just waiting to be picked. All I need is to see that smile on your face each morning, and know that when I go to bed at night, I'll be able to hold you in my arms. That's what'll make *me* happy."

"Then it's a deal," Molly said, and savored the sweep of his hands across her tears. And then she remembered the audience they'd left out front. She would bet a week's profit that not a one of them had left. "Oh Lord, what will those people out front think?"

"That we've been making out?"

She grinned and poked him in the rib. "Joseph! You don't understand!"

"Understand what, honey? You're making a big deal out of nothing. Everyone knows that it's impossible to resist temptation in the Garden of Eden."

"I think I've just been had," Molly said.

Joseph's eyes sparkled. The dimple she so loved deepened perceptibly. "You sure were," he whispered, and kissed the spot below her left ear. "And if we can lose 'Nanny' by midnight tonight, I promise that you'll be 'had' again . . . and again . . . and again."

Molly grinned. It was a promise she'd make him keep.

The World of Sharon Sala

When a man meets a woman in the books of Sharon Sala, there is no question that it is meant to be—that it is *fate*. For in the wonderful world of this bestselling author, who also writes as Dinah McCall, love is often left in the hands of destiny—threatening danger, the bonds of family, a terrible accident, or even just the whims of Mother Nature. Now, experience the romance for yourself, with these excerpts from a few of Sharon Sala's classic stories. Whether first love remembered or a new passion like no other, her stories will inspire your faith in destiny, and remind you that love is always around the next corner . . .

Chance McCall

*In one of Sharon Sala's most emotional love stories,
amnesia takes* Chance McCall *away from innocent
Jennifer Ann Tyler, who has been secretly in love with
him for as long as she can remember. When Chance re-
turns to her father's ranch, remembering nothing,
Jenny knows it's up to her to help speed Chance's re-
covery—and perhaps heal her broken heart at the same
time.*

Chance watched Jenny flit from one group of men
to the other, playing hostess one minute, and re-
verting to "one of the boys" the next. She kept
slipping glances in his direction when she
thought he wasn't looking, but, true to her claim,
she'd more or less left him alone. He didn't know
whether he was relieved or disappointed. His fingers curled around the cold bottle of beer in his
hand and knew that holding that beer was not
what he wanted to do. Holding Jenny seemed
much more necessary . . . and important.

"What's for dessert?" Henry asked, as Jenny
scraped the last of the potato salad onto his plate.

"Movies," she answered, and grinned at the

289

men's cheers of delight. "Roll 'em, Henry," she called as she walked away from Chance. "And the first one to start a fight has to clean up the party mess."

Chance grinned as the men muttered under their breaths. Jenny knew them well. They'd rather feed pigs than do "woman's work." And a cowboy does not willingly set foot around a pig.

Images danced through the night on the beam of light from the projector and jumped onto the screen, bringing a portion of the past to life. It didn't take long for the laughter to follow, as Henry's weathered face and hitched gait filled the screen.

He as leading a horse toward Jenny, who sat perched on the top rail of the corral. The smile on her face kicked Chance in the gut. And when she vaulted off the fence and threw her arms first around Henry, and then around the horse's neck, he swallowed harshly. It was a Jenny he'd never seen. This one wasn't scolding, or wearing a continual frown of worry. She was unconscious of her beauty, unconcerned with her clothing, and looked to be in her teens.

Firecrackers went off beneath a bystander's feet, telling Chance that it must have been a Fourth of July celebration that was being filmed. A man walked into the picture, and Jenny's face lit up like a roman candle. Absolute and total devotion was obvious. When the man turned around and made a face at the camera, Chance caught his breath. *It's me!* He had no memory at all of the occasion. Jenny was handing him a bridle that he slipped over the horse's head. She was smiling and laughing and clapping her hands as the crowd around her began singing.

It took Chance a minute to decipher the song, since this movie had no sound. Happy Birthday! They were singing Happy Birthday to Jenny! His breathing quickened and he stiffened as he watched Jenny throw her arms around his neck and plant a swift kiss on his cheek before allowing him to help her mount the horse. Because he was looking for it . . . because subconsciously he'd always known it was there . . . he didn't miss the intense look of love that Jenny gave him before she turned to the horse's head and rode off amid cheers and birthday greetings from the crowd.

It was too much! Chance knew that the rest of the night would simply be a rerun of similar scenes and similar people. He didn't have to remember it to know that Jenny Tyler loved him. He'd felt it through the darkness in the hospital, when he had no memory at all . . . when there was nothing in his life but misery and pain.

What he didn't know, and what he couldn't face, was the depth of his own feelings for the boss's daughter, and memory of what, if anything, had ever happened between them. He turned and walked away, hidden by night shadows.

Jenny saw him go and resisted an urge to cry. It would do no good. And it would be too obvious if she bolted after him. *Damn this all to hell*, she thought. *Why can't you remember me, Chance McCall? Injury or not, I'd have to be dead not to remember you.*

Second Chances

Weather stranded both Billie and Matt in the same airport, but it was fate that made them meet in Second Chances. After disastrous holidays, Billie Jean finds herself trapped in Memphis on New Year's Eve. She is alone, until she meets a tall cowboy lingering in the shadows and passion takes over. What seems like a fluke is really the hand of destiny, changing Billie's and Matt's lives forever.

Matt sensed, rather than heard, her approach, as if someone had invaded his space without asking. Instinctively he shifted his absent gaze from the swirling snow outside to the reflection of the woman he saw coming toward him from the rear.

At first, she was nothing more than a tall, dark shadow. It was hard to tell exactly how much woman was concealed beneath the long, bulky sweater she wore, but she had a slow, lanky stride that made his belly draw in an unexpected ache. Just as he was concentrating on slim hips encased in tight denim and telling himself he'd rather be alone, she spoke.

"Would you like something to drink?"

Every thought he had came to a stop as her voice wrapped around his senses. Men called it a bedroom voice—a low, husky drawl that made his toes curl and his breath catch.

But when their hands touched, Matt wasn't the only one in a state of sudden confusion. Billie lost her train of thought, while the smile on her lips froze like the snow against the windows. There was a look in his eyes that she'd never before seen on a man's face. A mystery, an intensity in the dark blue gaze that she hadn't bargained for. Several staggering breaths later, she remembered what she'd been about to say.

"I thought you might like to . . ."

She never got to finish what she was saying. He took the can and set it down on the ledge without taking his eyes off her face. Mesmerized, she stood without moving as his hands lifted toward her cheeks. When his fingers sifted through the strands of escaping curls that were falling around her eyes, she caught herself leaning toward his touch and jerked back in shock. Then he grinned, and she felt herself relaxing once more.

He lifted a stray curl from the corner of her eye. "That face is too pretty to hide."

A surge of pure joy made Billie weak at the knees. Embarrassed, she looked away, and when she looked back, found herself locked into a wild, stormy gaze and dealing with another sort of surge. Ashamed of what she was thinking, she pretended interest in the storm and knew that she was blushing.

"Where are you going?"

I wish to hell it was with you. Wisely, Matt kept his wishes to himself.

"Dallas."

She nodded and looked down at the floor.

"I was in Memphis for Christmas vacation. I'm on my way back to California." When she got the nerve to look up, those dark blue eyes were still staring intently.

They shared a long, silent moment, then the noise of the crowd behind them broke the tension. It was obvious by the loud chanting voices that the countdown to midnight had begun.

"Ten . . . nine . . . eight."

Billie looked up. His eyes were so blue. So compelling. So lonely. She took a deep breath.

"Seven . . . six . . . five."

She bit her lower lip, then took a step forward. Just in case. Hoping—wishing—needing him to want what she was wanting.

"Four . . . three . . . two."

Matt groaned beneath his breath. He saw the invitation in her eyes as well as her body language. So help him God, there wasn't enough strength left in him to deny either of them the obvious.

The merrymakers were in full swing as they shouted, "Happy New Year!"

Matt cupped her face in his hands, then waited. If she didn't want this, now was her chance to move. To his utter joy, she not only stayed but scooted a hair-breadth closer to his chest until he could almost feel the gentle jut of her breasts against the front of his shirt. Almost . . . but not quite.

"Happy New Year, Memphis." He lowered his head.

Finders Keepers

Molly Eden thinks fate is not on her side. Ever since her chance at a baby was robbed from her, grief has only been a few steps behind. Then, on a warm summer day, someone comes toddling into her life to change it forever. Joseph Rossi's baby son Joey is that darling someone, and when Joey Jr. asks Molly to be his mother, he proves that children can be wise beyond their years and see love where there was only loneliness before in Finders Keepers.

"Isth you my momma?"

Molly didn't know what startled her more, the unexpected question or the touch of a child's hand on her bare thigh.

"What in the world?"

She spun. The food on her barbecue and her solitary picnic were forgotten as she stared down in shock at the small boy who waited patiently for an answer to his question. She was startled by the unexpected pain of his innocent question—it had been years since she'd let herself think of being anyone's momma. But the child's expression was just short of panicked, and his hand was warm—so warm—upon her thigh; she couldn't ignore his plight just because of her old ghosts.

"Hey there, fella, where did you come from?" Molly bent down, and when he offered no resistance, she lifted him into her arms.

But he had no answers for Molly, only an increase in the tug of his tongue against the thumb he had stuffed in his mouth. She smiled at his intense expression, and patted his chubby bare legs. Except for a pair of small red shorts, an expression was the *only* thing he was wearing.

"Where did you come from, sweetheart?"

His chin quivered and then he tugged a little faster upon his thumb.

It was obvious to Molly that the child was not going to be any help in locating missing parents. She turned, searching her spacious backyard for something or someone to explain the child's appearance, but nothing was obviously different from the way it had been for the last twenty-two years when her parents first moved in—except the child.

"Are you lost, honey? Can't you find your mommy?"

His only response was a limpid look from chocolate-chip eyes that nearly melted her on the spot.

She frowned, patting his sticky back in a comforting but absent way and started toward the house to call the police when shouts from the yard next door made her pause.

"Joey! Joey, where are you? Answer me, son!"

Even through the eight-foot height of the thick yew hedge separating the homes, Molly could hear the man's panic. She looked down at the child in her arms and sighed with relief. If she wasn't mistaken, the missing parents were about to arrive, and from a surprise location. The house on the adjoining lot had been vacant for over a year, and she'd been unaware that anyone had moved next door.

"Hey! You over there . . . are you missing a small boy?"

"Yes . . . God, yes, please tell me you found him."

Molly smiled with relief as she realized her unexpected guest was about to be retrieved. "He's here!" she shouted again. "You can come around the hedge and then through the front door of my house. It's unlocked."

The thrashing sounds in the bushes next door ceased. Molly imagined she could hear his labored breathing as the man tried to regain a sense of stability in a world that had gone awry. But she knew it was not her imagination when she heard

299

a long, slow, string of less-than-silent curses fill the air. Relief had obviously replaced the father's panic.

Molly raised her eyebrows at the man's colorful language, but got no response from the child in her arms. He didn't look too perturbed. But he did remove his thumb from his mouth long enough to remark, "My daddy," before stuffing it back in place.

"Well, really!" Molly said, more in shock for herself than for the child, who had obviously heard it all before.

She turned toward the patio door, expecting the arrival of just an ordinary man, and then found herself gaping at the male who bolted out of her door and onto her patio.

It had been a long time since she'd been struck dumb by a physical attraction, but it was there just the same, as blatant and shocking as it could possibly be. All she could think to do was take a deep breath to regain her equilibrium and then wave a welcome. That in itself took no effort, and it was much safer than the thoughts that came tumbling through her mind.

She saw the man pause on the threshold, as if taking a much-needed breath, and then swipe a shaky hand across his face. He was tall, muscular, and, oddly enough, quite wet. His hair lay back and seal-slick against his head like a short, dark cap, while droplets of water beaded across his shoulders.

He stared at her backside and then tried not to. But it was an impossible task. Her long, tan legs made short work of the distance to the grill. He tried to remember his manners as he followed behind.

Deep in the Heart

In Deep in the Heart, *it is danger that brings Samantha Carlyle back to her rural Texas hometown, and back into the world of John Thomas Knight, the stunning local sheriff. She left him behind once for the bright lights and big city, but the success she found there—or the threats that came with it—is exactly what brings her into his arms again . . .*

There were no tears left to cry. Unmitigated terror had become commonplace for Samantha Carlyle. She was waiting for the inevitable. Day by day the stalker came closer, and there was nothing she could do to stop him.

She could barely remember her life three months ago when she'd been a highly valued member of a Hollywood casting agency, calmly and competently going about the business of fitting the famous and the not-so-famous into starring and supporting roles.

"And look at you now," Samantha whispered to her own reflection as she stood in the window overlooking the courtyard below. "You have no job. You're running from the devil and your own shadow. You're just hiding . . . and waiting to die."

Until now, she'd never considered what it meant to be "living on borrowed time." She looked again at her reflection and wondered what there was about her that could drive a man to insane threats of vengeance.

Her face was no different from many others—heartshaped, but a bit too thin, and framed by a mane of thick, black hair. Her nose was still small and turned up at the world, but there was no longer a jut to her chin. It only trembled. Her lips were full but colorless, and the life that had once shone from her eyes seemed dim . . . almost gone. She shuddered and dropped the drapes, rearranging them to shut the sun out and herself in from prying eyes.

When the harassment had gone from hate mail to phone calls with spine-chilling messages left in an unrecognizable voice, she'd nearly lost her mind and, soon after, she did lose her so-called friends.

As if that wasn't enough, she'd moved her residence twice, certain each time she would outwit the culprit. And then came the day that she realized she was being stalked. But by then going back to the police was out of the question. They had convinced themselves that she was concocting the incidents herself. In fact, they had almost convinced her.

Her anger at their accusations had quickly turned to disbelief when they had proved to her, without doubt, that the hate letters she'd been receiving had been typed on her own office typewriter, and that the calls left on her answering machine were traced to an empty apartment that had been rented in the name of Samantha Jean Carlyle. It was enough said. When LAPD reminded her that perpetrating fraud was a crime, she'd taken her letters and her tapes and gone home, having decided to hire a personal bodyguard. Then she'd reconsidered her financial situation and given up on that idea.

That was the day her boss put her on indefinite leave of absence, after reminding her, of course, that when she got her act together she would be welcomed back.

The victim had become the accused. At first she'd been furious over everyone's lack of sympathy for her situation or concern for her life. Then she'd become too busy trying to stay alive.

It was the constant frustration and the growing fear that no one was going to save her, let alone believe her, that made her remember Johnny Knight.

Touchstone

In Touchstone, *a Dinah McCall classic, fate doesn't bring two lovers together, but instead tries to tear them apart. Rachel Austin has buried her father, and now her mother, and finally they are coming for her family's land. She cannot bear staying in Mirage, where all she'd ever known is lost, but she soon discovers that without her first—and only—love, Houston Bookout, she will never stared down the demons of her past. Look for* Touchstone *in reissue from HarperTorch December 2003.*

"Rachel!"

He heard fear in his own voice and took a deep breath, making himself calm. But when she didn't answer, the fear kicked itself up another notch.

"Rachel! Where are you?"

He started toward the house, then something—call it instinct—made him turn. She came toward him out of the darkness, a slender shadow moving through the perimeter of light from his headlamps, then centering itself in the beam. She was still wearing the clothes she had on this morning, when he'd seen her last: worn-out Levi's and an old denim shirt. She came toward him without speaking. Fear slid from him, leaving him weak and shaken.

"Damn it, Cherokee, you scared me to death. Why didn't you answer me? Better yet, what the hell are you still doing here in the dark?"

Then he saw her face and knew she was incapable of answering.

"Jesus." He opened his arms.

She walked into them without saying a word and buried her face in the middle of his chest.

He rocked her where they stood, wrapping his fingers in the thickness of her hair and feeling her body tremble against his.

"It's going to be all right," he said softly. "I promise you, girl, it's going to be all right."

She shook her head. "No, Houston. It will never be all right again. It's gone. Everything is gone. First my father. Then my mother. Now they're taking my home."

He ached for her. "I know, love, I know. But I'm still here. I'll never leave you."

But it was as if he'd never spoken.

"The land . . . they always take the land," she muttered, and dropped to her knees. Silhouetted by the headlights of Houston's truck, she thrust her hands in the dirt and started to shake.

Houston knelt beside her. "Rachel . . ."

She didn't blink, staring instead at the way the dust began to trickle through her fingers.

"How can I give this up? It's where I was born. It's where my parents are buried."

He didn't have words to ease her pain.

She rocked back on her heels and stood abruptly. Fury colored her movements and her words.

"Everything is over! Over! And all because of money."

Houston reached for her, but she spun away. A knot formed in Houston's gut. He grabbed for her again, and this time when she tried to shake herself free, he tightened his hold.

"Stop it!" he said sharply, and gripped her by both shoulders. "Look at me, Rachel."

She wouldn't.

He shook harder. "Damn it! I said look at me!"

Finally, reluctantly, she met his gaze. She saw concern and anger; to her despair, she saw fear and knew it was because of her. She went limp.

"Houston."

He groaned and pulled her to him. "Damn it, Cherokee, don't turn away from me, too."

She shuddered. Cherokee. She couldn't deny

her heritage any more than she could deny her love for Houston.

"I'm sorry," she whispered.

"It doesn't matter," he said. "Nothing matters but you."

He took her by the hand.

"Wait . . . my car," Rachel muttered.

"Leave it," he said. "You're coming home with me."

"But the sale. I need to be here by seven."

Houston frowned. "I'll have you here by sunup if it'll make you happy. But you're still coming home with me."

They made the drive back to his ranch in total silence.

Rachel felt numb from the inside out until she walked in the front door of Houston's home. The odors of cleaning solutions and pine-scented furniture polish were startling. She inhaled sharply, and as she did, tears blurred her vision. He'd been cleaning for her. Her anger dimmed as shame swept over her. She turned.

"Oh, Houston."

"Come here, girl. Don't fight your last friend."

She shuddered as his arms went around her. Last friend? If he only knew. He was her best and last friend, and in a couple of days he was going to hate her guts. A sob worked its way up her throat, but she wouldn't give in. No time to cry. Not when she wanted to remember.

She tilted her head to look up at him. "Make love to me, Houston. Make me forget."

Chase the Moon

Chase the Moon *will always be remembered as one of Sharon Sala's—here writing as Dinah McCall—most passionate, thrilling stories of love. When Jake Baretta goes looking for his twin brother's killer, he finds instead beautiful Gracie Moon—a woman he could easily fall for, if only she didn't believe he was his dead brother. Sheltered and innocent, Gracie doesn't know about the evil that lurks under the surface of her idealistic Kentucky hometown—but she is in danger of find out, far too soon. Look for* Chase the Moon *in reissue from HarperTorch December 2003.*

Less than an hour later, Jake was startled by a knock on the door, but even more so by the woman behind it.

All Gracie said was, "Oh, Jake," and then walked into his arms.

He froze and tried not to panic. *Damn, Johnny, why didn't you warn me this would happen?*

Her arms were around his waist, her cheek against his chest, and he felt her shoulders trembling. Her long dark braid felt heavy against his

310

hands as he tentatively returned her embrace. The thrust of her breasts, the feel of her slender body against his, were startling. He hadn't prepared himself for this, or for the supposition that John could have had a personal relationship with anyone here—no less with a woman as damned beautiful as this one. Worst of all, she thought he was John.

It took a moment for Jake's shock to pass. He didn't know who she was, but he suspected that this was Elijah Moon's only daughter. From the files he'd read, Gracie Moon was the only unattached female in New Zion. He hoped to God this was Gracie, because if John had been seeing a married woman, then that would pretty much explain why he had been shot.

He said a prayer and took a chance.

"Gracie?"

Gracie sighed. She loved to hear her name on his lips, and then she remembered herself and took a quick step back. There were tears in her eyes as she laid her hands on his shoulders.

"Father said you'd been shot." Her chin trembled, and she bit her lip to keep from crying. "He said you didn't trust us anymore." Tears hovered on the edge of her lashes. "Does that mean you don't trust me, either?"

Jake stifled a groan. My God, how could he answer her? For all he knew, she could be the one who'd pulled the trigger. Just because she was beautiful as sin, and just because there were tears in her eyes, did not make her an innocent woman. But he had to play the game. It was why he'd come.

"I guess what it means is, getting shot in the back put me off balance. Trust isn't something that's happening yet. But I'm glad to see you, too. Does that count?"

Gracie ducked her head, fighting tears, and when she looked up, there was a sad smile on her face.

"Of course it counts," she said softly.

She kept looking at him. At his eyes. At the shape of his mouth. At the cut of his chin. Finally, she shrugged.

"You look the same . . . but in a way you're very different. Harder, even colder." A gentle smile accompanied her apology. "But I suppose surviving being shot in the back would do that to anyone, right?"

"It made me hate," Jake answered.

Gracie touched his arm. "Just don't hate me."